Feeling a little better, Reggie started slowly shifting in his arms. She was becoming far too aware of how perfect his torso was, how he smelled of that deep, earthy spice that had always been intoxicating to her senses, and how she wanted nothing more than to ease back, lift her head and have him press his lips to hers.

He'd done it time and time again in the past, and as his arms loosened, allowing her to shift a little more, she couldn't help but look up at him. His gaze automatically dipped to take in the contours of her mouth, and the atmosphere between them changed from one of supportive colleagues to one of experienced familiarity.

She looked into his gorgeous eyes, hooded by those gorgeous long lashes, at his straight nose, his cleft chin and his slightly parted mouth. His arms were no longer protective and supportive but instead were bands of warmth, heating her up all over. Didn't the man have any idea just how powerful his hold was over her? She wanted him to kiss her, to follow through on the urge which seemed to be so tangible between them you could cut it with a knife.

Dear Reader

Funny and vivacious Reggie has been waiting patiently for me to tell her story, and here it is—the last in the *Sunshine General* series. She's woven her way in and out of stories about her close friends, Mackenzie, Bergan and Sunainah, and now her three friends are right there with her as they watch her fall in love with the fabulous Flynn, clapping and cheering all the way.

These four friends have overcome so much adversity, and I like the way that although they're all very different they have such a tight bond, accepting each other for who they are and simply showing each other love. Friendships are vitally important, it's true, but the other thing I love about these four women are the four men who enter their lives and turn their worlds upside down. Flynn is no different, with the way he bursts back into Reggie's life, clearly still attracted to her and wanting to show her just how much he's changed for the better.

Flynn, John, Elliot and Richard I know will also become the best of friends, throwing another shrimp on the barbecue during their cul-de-sac crew gatherings, whilst their wives, Reggie, Mackenzie, Sunainah and Bergan, sit back with a relaxing glass of wine and toast their friendship.

I do hope you've enjoyed the *Sunshine General* series—spreading a little sunshine!

Warmest regards

Lucy

HER MISTLETOE WISH

BY
LUCY CLARK

First published in Great Britain 2013
by Mills & Boon, an imprint of Harlequin (UK) Limited.
Harlequin (UK) Limited, Eton House, 18-24 Paradise Road,
Richmond, Surrey TW9 1SR

© Anne Clark & Peter Clark 2013

ISBN: 978 0 263 23389 6

enewable
;ustainable
to the

Lucy Clark is actually a husband-and-wife writing team. They enjoy taking holidays with their children, during which they discuss and develop new ideas for their books using the fantastic Australian scenery. They use their daily walks to talk over characterisation and fine details of the wonderful stories they produce, and are avid movie buffs. They live on the edge of a popular wine district in South Australia with their two children, and enjoy spending family time together at weekends.

Recent titles by Lucy Clark:

THE SECRET BETWEEN THEM
RESISTING THE NEW DOC IN TOWN
ONE LIFE CHANGING MOMENT
DARE SHE DREAM OF FOREVER?
FALLING FOR DR FEARLESS
DIAMOND RING FOR THE ICE QUEEN
TAMING THE LONE DOC'S HEART
THE BOSS SHE CAN'T RESIST
WEDDING ON THE BABY WARD
SPECIAL CARE BABY MIRACLE
DOCTOR: DIAMOND IN THE ROUGH

These books are also available in eBook format from www.millsandboon.co.uk

For Melva. You're never too old to make a new friend,
and I'm glad I'm one of yours.
You are a very special person to my mother,
my daughter and to me.
Thank you for sharing your 'wisdom'.
Let's put the kettle on...
Pr 1:7

CHAPTER ONE

REGGIE SMITH RACED into the outpatient clinic, smiling and waving to the patients who were awaiting her attention. The clinic was decorated with tinsel and baubles and a sad-looking branch from a gum tree had been potted in the corner, dressed with twinkle lights in an effort to add a bit of festive cheer to the people waiting to see the doctor.

Christmas was Reggie's favourite time of year because it always brought hope and she was a big believer in hope. Plus, in the weeks leading up to Christmas, everyone seemed to be in a happier mood, calling a quick 'Have a great Christmas' or 'Merry Christmas' or 'Happy holidays'. Of course, Sunshine General Hospital was also abuzz with the annual hospital auction to be held ten days before Christmas and as Reggie was part of the organising committee, there was still much to do.

'Four weeks until Christmas and I haven't even started my shopping,' one of her closest friends, Mackenzie, had said to her only yesterday as they'd finalised the venue for the hospital auction.

'I'm almost done.' Reggie had grinned widely.

'Show-off,' Mackenzie had returned.

Even thinking about it made Reggie smile as she screeched to a halt at the outpatient clinic desk. 'Sorry,

sorry,' she called brightly. 'I was held up in A and E. Sorry, sorry.' Her words were genuine as she honestly didn't like to keep people waiting but sometimes, especially where she was concerned, time seemed to have a habit of disappearing.

'It's just like you, Reggie.' Clara, the clerk, smiled as she pointed to a bundle of case notes, indicating they were Reggie's patients for the morning. 'Luckily, the new general surgeon covering Geetha's maternity leave has already started the clinic so you shouldn't be too far behind.'

'I didn't think Geetha was leaving for another week,' Reggie said as she hefted the notes into her arms.

'Handover period,' Clara offered. 'Don't you ever read your emails?'

Reggie's answer was to grin and shrug. 'You know me!' She looked at the top name on the case notes in her arms. 'Er…Mr Searle. Would you like to come on through?'

She waited while Mr Searle, an elderly man in his sixties, stood and started walking towards her, barely leaning on the walking stick in his right hand.

'You're walking really well,' she said, clearly impressed as the two of them walked slowly down the corridor towards her consulting room. 'I spoke to Mackenzie, your orthopaedic surgeon, the other day and she told me how pleased she was with your progress. After today's check-up, you might be able to get a break from this place for a while.'

'I'm looking forward to it,' Mr Searle replied as he headed through into her consulting room. 'No offence intended,' he added.

'None taken,' she remarked, waving her hand in the air with a dramatic flourish. 'I love it when my patients

are well enough to get back to living their normal lives.'
Her eyes were alive with delight, her voice filled with
happiness, but as she turned to close her consulting-
room door, the door directly opposite hers opened.

The smile slowly slid from Reggie's face, her eyes
widened in shock, and her jaw dropped open in disbelief as Flynn Jamieson—*the Flynn Jamieson*—stood
opposite her. He was dressed in a pair of navy trousers,
a crisp white shirt and striped university tie. His hands
were on his hips as he stared at her with his piercing
blue eyes.

'Do you have to be so noisy, Reg?'

At the use of the familiar name, especially as he
was the only person she'd ever allowed to call her that,
Reggie's eyes flashed with fire as annoyance replaced
surprise. 'Please don't call me that. Excuse me.' With
that, she closed her consulting-room door, effectively
shutting out the sight of him.

She leaned against the door and closed her eyes for a
moment, unable to ignore the repressed pulsing desire,
the one only Flynn could evoke, and the way her entire
body seemed to be trembling just from the sight of him.
What on earth was Flynn Jamieson doing here? In Australia? In Queensland? In Maroochydore? In Sunshine
General Hospital—*her* hospital?

No sooner had the questions started running around
in her head than the answer materialised like magic.
'Surgeon covering Geetha's maternity leave,' she whispered. Why, oh, why hadn't she read her emails? The
head of the surgery department was a great communi-
cator, always keeping the surgical staff informed with
the latest happenings, but it was Reggie who was the
bad receiver of these communications, which meant

she really had no one else to blame but herself for being shocked at Flynn's appearance.

'Reggie?' Mr Searle's voice brought her attention back to the present and she quickly opened her eyes and pasted on a smile, forcing herself to push all thoughts of the disturbing Flynn Jamieson to the back of her mind. So what if he was here? So what if she would be required to work with him? She'd worked with him before and they'd made a good professional team. The fact that he'd broken her heart six years ago meant nothing to her now. *He* meant nothing to her now. Nothing at all.

'Sorry, Mr Searle.' Reggie dragged in a breath and placed the pile of case notes on the desk, taking Mr Searle's from the top and opening them up as she sat down in the chair. 'Let's get your examination under-way.'

For the rest of the Monday morning outpatient clinic Reggie did her utmost to avoid any and all contact with Flynn, forcing herself to focus on being her usual bright and cheerful self for the sake of her patients. They deserved nothing less but once her last patient for the morning had exited her consulting room, Reggie immediately picked up the receiver of the internal hospital phone and called Mackenzie.

'It's Reggie,' she stated before Mackenzie could even squeeze out a 'hello'. 'We have to meet. Are you free? Coffee shop across the road from the hospital in ten minutes?'

'I think I can do that. What's wrong, Reggie?'

'The worst thing possible.'

'What?'

Reggie could hear the worry in Mackenzie's voice but it was nothing compared to the utter panic and devastation in her own. 'It's Flynn. He's *here*!'

* * *

'This is an emergency,' Reggie told her friends fifteen minutes later as they all sat round a table, sipping coffee.

'I cannot believe Flynn is back,' Sunainah said, her sparkling new wedding rings gleaming brightly on her left hand. Reggie tried not to look at them, or Bergan's, or Mackenzie's. During the past eighteen months, all three of her closest friends had found their true loves and were now happily married. She had tried not to let it bother her, had tried to remain as happy and as optimistic as she'd always been, but deep down inside, late at night when she was all alone in her apartment, she had curled into a tight little ball and cried, feeling incredibly lonely.

And now, to top everything off, Flynn Jamieson was back in her life. He was the only man she had ever truly given her heart to, the only man she had ever truly loved, and yet he was the only man who had ever truly crushed her beyond despair.

'What are you going to do?' Bergan asked.

'What do you mean, what am I going to do? I'm going to yell and scream and bellyache and do my best not to fall apart in front of him. I mean…' She spread her arms wide as she slumped back in her chair. 'It's *Flynn*.' Reggie closed her eyes. '*My* Flynn,' she whispered, as Mackenzie put her arms around Reggie and hugged her close.

'How did he look?' Bergan asked.

Reggie sighed and shook her head as though she were a completely lost cause. 'Good. *Really* good.'

'But he is not married anymore, is that correct?' Sunainah asked.

Reggie sighed and looked at her friends. 'Not as far as I know, but then, I stopped reading the latest society gossip of the rich and famous after I saw the picture of him and his blonde, buxom bride splashed across the front pages. A man does not break off an engagement with one woman and then marry another in under a fortnight.' She glared at her untouched coffee, her voice as dark as the beverage.

Less than twenty-four hours after Flynn had taken her out to a romantic restaurant, given her red roses, plied her with the finest champagne and then strolled with her along the beach at sunset, stopping momentarily to go down on bended knee to not only confess his love for her but profess that it was *she* he wanted to spend the rest of his life with—he'd come round to her apartment and called the whole thing off, telling her it had been a mistake.

'Stupid romance. Stupid rich people. Stupid Flynn,' she grumbled, her frown deepening. 'And I thought I was going to have a good Christmas this year. Fat chance of that happening now.' She sighed, trying to figure out how she was supposed to deal with working alongside him every day until Geetha returned from maternity leave, which could be anywhere from six to twelve months from now.

Lifting her gaze from scowling at her coffee, it was then Reggie noticed that her three friends were giving each other very worried looks. They'd all known each other so well, for so many years, having been through so much together, that sometimes there was no need for words to communicate exactly what they were thinking.

They'd met at medical school, all of them having come from very different backgrounds, but their past adversities had been the one thing that had ended up binding them together. None of them had had an easy ride throughout their life but in looking out for each other and offering constant support, they'd formed their own family unit. So Reggie could easily read their expressions and she shook her head.

'I'm not going to fall for him again. I can tell that's what you're all thinking, aren't you,' she stated rhetorically.

'Well…' Sunainah shrugged.

'You've always said he was your one true love,' Mackenzie added.

'I'm more worried about you turning into a crazy nutter again,' Bergan added, her words matter-of-fact but filled with love. 'I mean, after you broke up you not only removed every single trace of Flynn from your life, destroying and disposing of all the very expensive gifts he'd given you, but you cut your hair super-short, coloured it purple and threw yourself into matchmaking your friends.'

'Well, I can't do the last bit anymore,' Reggie pointed out, indicating the wedding rings her friends were wearing, then added thoughtfully, 'I could possibly colour my hair again. I've always wanted to go green. What do you think? Green streaks?'

Before her friends could answer, Bergan's and Mackenzie's phones rang. They quickly answered them and while they spoke, Sunainah reached across the table and took Reggie's hand in hers.

'Just…pause, Reggie. Stop and take a breath.' Sunainah's phone started buzzing with a reminder and she shook her head. 'I am sorry, Reggie. My clinic will be starting in five minutes. I need to—'

'Go.' Reggie waved her hands towards her friends, shooing them away. 'Thanks for giving me probably the only fifteen minutes you had spare. I do appreciate it.'

'Sorry,' Mackenzie said, as she and Bergan stood.

'Emergency,' Bergan added.

'My afternoon theatre list will be starting late so call me if I'm needed to help out,' Reggie told Bergan.

'Will do,' her friend replied.

Reggie picked up her coffee, sipping it as she watched her friends finish their drinks quickly and head back to the hospital. She prided herself on always being happy, always having a bright smile on her face, a genuine smile, one that would bring happiness to others. Forever optimistic—that's what her friends had called her, yet now she wanted to wallow in her despondency, blaming Flynn Jamieson for making her feel this way.

'Definitely green hair,' she mumbled to herself a few minutes later, unable to lift herself out of her grumpy mood.

'I think it would look great,' a deep male voice said from behind her, a voice she instantly recognised and one that set her entire body alight with sparks of joy and excitement. Reggie turned round to look over her shoulder but didn't see him. Had she imagined it? Was she going insane, thinking every deep male voice belonged to Flynn?

She turned her attention back to her drink and almost jumped with fright when she saw Flynn lowering his six-foot-four-inch frame into the chair opposite her. She quickly put her coffee back onto the table before she spilled it. 'Don't do that, Flynn. You know I don't like being scared.'

He nodded. 'I do. Sorry. Couldn't resist.'

'Try.' She glared at him suspiciously. 'How long have you been lurking around here?' She indicated the immediate vicinity around her table. Had he overheard them all talking?

'I came in as your friends were leaving. I received a very cool look from…Bergan, is it?'

'Yes.' She frowned. 'How did you know that?'

'You showed me quite a few pictures of all your friends during our time together in the Caribbean. Don't you remember?'

Reggie sat up straighter in her chair, squaring her shoulders. 'I can't remember a lot of things about the Caribbean. It was so long ago.' She tried to inflect a touch of nonchalance into her tone but could tell from the disbelieving look on his face that he wasn't really buying it.

Flynn nodded slowly then just sat there, staring at her as though he was drinking in the sight of her. 'How have you been, Reg?'

She gritted her teeth at his familiarity, not wanting to give him the satisfaction again of seeing how the intimate name flustered her. 'I'm…fine.'

'Freaked out? Insecure? Neurotic and emotional?' he checked, and she shook her head in annoyance.

'Don't be cute, Flynn.'

He spread his arms wide and leaned back in his chair. 'I don't know how to be any other way.' His smile was big, his eyebrows were raised and his twinkling eyes were clearly teasing her.

'I see your arrogance is still in check.'

He surprised her by chuckling and she instantly wished he hadn't, the warm, inviting sound washing over her like a comfortable blanket. She'd always loved his laugh, always loved making him laugh, but not like this, not through silly barbs and jibes.

Reggie bit her tongue, needing to get her ridiculous hormones under control, to remain cool, calm and collected. 'What are you doing here?

'In the coffee shop?'

She levelled him with a glare. 'Flynn.' There was warning in her tone.

'Oh. At Sunshine General? I'm covering Geetha's maternity leave.'

'So I gathered but…er…' How did she ask this without sounding self-important? 'Did you know I was working at Sunshine General?'

Flynn didn't answer her but instead checked his watch. 'We're going to be late for afternoon theatre if we don't get a move on.'

'I don't care,' she continued to grump as Flynn stood. He obviously hadn't been told the morning elective theatre lists had run overtime. She watched as he shoved his hands into the pockets of his trousers and stared down at her with that crazy little smile touching the corners of his lips. It was a smile that had never failed to set her heart racing and now was no exception.

'You're sounding like Scrooge, Reggie.'

'Bah, humbug,' she muttered as she finished her now-cold coffee and stood. She didn't really want to walk back to the hospital with Flynn because even being this close to him was already causing her body to react with all the hallmarks of years gone past. Her heart was beating wildly, her mouth was dry, her knees were shaking and she momentarily leaned on the table for support.

'How can *you* not be in the Christmas spirit? You, who always wanted it to be Christmas all year round? The woman who loved wishing everyone happy holidays as she walked around the hospital or went to the shops or the gym or, in fact, anywhere.' Flynn pressed a finger to his lips in thought.

'In fact, I remember you animatedly and jovially wishing the Prince of the Netherlands the happiest

Christmas one year. Then the next day you gave a home-less man the same greeting in exactly the same way.' He shook his head in bemusement. 'That's one thing I always liked about you, Reggie. You treated every-one, prince or pauper, the same. You afford everyone the same courtesy.'

Reggie glared at Flynn, her anger beginning to rise. 'Don't compliment me.'

'Why not?'

Her mind tried to think of a reason because she could hardly tell him that his words had warmed her heart. She didn't want her heart to be warmed by Flynn. Not now. Not ever. But he was still standing there, waiting for her reply. 'Just…because.' She shook her head and walked out of the café, waving her thanks to the owner and managing to muster a half-hearted smile. She hated herself for feeling this way, for not spreading joy and happiness, as was her wont, but seeing Flynn again, even walking alongside him as he fell into step beside her was throwing her completely off balance.

'Just because? What kind of answer is that?'

'The only one you're going to get.' She pressed the button at the pedestrian crossing with great impatience, wanting the light to turn green instantly so she could walk away from the man who had hurt her so bitterly. Still, she wasn't the same woman she'd been six years ago. Once more in her life she'd been forced to pick herself up and keep moving forward. His rejection of her had only served to make her stronger and because of that she could and would stand up to him.

Drawing in a deep breath, she turned to face him, to give him a piece of her mind, to tell him to leave her alone, but it was only then she became aware of other people coming to join them at the traffic lights, waiting to cross the road. She was forced to step closer to him, to rise on her toes so she could direct her words closer to his ear.

'Whatever happened between us happened a long time ago, Flynn.'

'It wasn't that long ago,' Flynn pointed out, stepping closer to her, dipping his head and heightening the repressed awareness she was experiencing. She closed her eyes, desperate to remain in control of the situation and not be swayed by the cologne he was wearing, the same scent she'd introduced him to all those years ago, assuring him the subtle spicy scent suited him much better than the woodsy one he'd been wearing. She couldn't believe he was still wearing the hypnotic, alluring scent.

The lights turned green, the beeping sound from the pedestrian crossing startling her slightly. She opened her eyes and belatedly realised that while everyone else had moved off, she and Flynn were just standing there, close—too close—looking at each other. She swallowed over her dry throat, desperate to ignore the tingles and sparkles and butterflies and all the other sensations this man had the habit of creating deep within her.

'It was another lifetime ago,' she eventually retorted, before turning and walking across the road, having to run the last little way as the flashing pedestrian sign had already turned red.

'It was a good lifetime, though.' His voice came from behind her and she glanced over her shoulder, not realising he'd crossed the road behind her. 'We had a good time together.'

'I don't want to talk about it.' She stopped walking for a moment and turned to glare at him. 'Why are you here? Why now? Why—?' She broke off, her voice cracking on the words. She looked away from him and shook her head, unable to believe her body and mind were betraying her by reacting to his enigmatic presence and becoming so emotional.

Swallowing, she shook her head and turned away from him, knowing it was better to beat a hasty retreat than say something she would regret. While Flynn may have broken her heart, it wasn't in her nature to be mean or malicious.

She didn't want to look behind her, didn't want to know whether or not Flynn was following her. She didn't want to know his whereabouts, she didn't want to work alongside him in the clinic and she didn't want to deal with him during operating lists. She wanted him to go, to leave the hospital and Maroochydore—in fact, leave Australia…and leave her alone.

So why, after the way he'd been smiling at her in the coffee shop, did she get the feeling that wasn't about to happen?

CHAPTER TWO

REGGIE WAS GLAD she had a busy theatre list to focus her thoughts. It was easier to push the reappearance of Flynn Jamieson in her life to the back of her mind and instead be calm and controlled as she removed Mr Philmott's gallbladder, relieved young Cynthia Schroder of her inflamed appendix and performed a hernia repair on Mrs Grant.

Between cases, she did her best not to run into Flynn, knowing he was operating in the next theatre. At one point, she was in the doctor's tearoom, just finishing a much-needed cup of coffee, when she thought she heard his voice out in the corridor. Panic filled her insides and as she glanced wildly around the room she realised there really was no place for her to hide.

Quickly washing her cup, she headed to the door, intent on slipping out of the room as he came in. Never had she been more grateful to Ingrid Brown, one of the general surgical registrars who had been assigned to assist Flynn in Theatre, because as they came into the tearoom Ingrid was intent on keeping Flynn's attention firmly on her.

'Reg?' Flynn interrupted Ingrid the instant he saw Reggie standing by the door. 'How's everything going in Theatre?'

'Great,' she offered, and quickly left the room, trying to ignore the spate of tingles that seemed to flood right through her body from the quick glance she'd received from Flynn. Why was it that even after six years, after breaking her heart and making her feel as though she was worthless, he could still create such havoc with her senses?

And that was the way things went for the next week, with Reggie doing her best to quickly slip out of a room the instant he walked in. Keeping a nice, uncomplicated distance between them was helping her to focus on her patients, on the planning for the hospital Christmas auction and on keeping her paperwork up to date. The fact that she was as jumpy as a long-tailed cat in a roomful of rocking chairs every time a nearby door opened or she heard male voices in the corridor meant nothing.

Self-preservation was of paramount importance in situations such as this, but even through all her efforts of avoidance she was having difficulty sleeping because the instant she lay in her bed and closed her eyes, memories of her past encounters with Flynn flooded her mind.

So many memories yet such a short time together. For the first two weeks in the Caribbean, she'd kept her distance from him, trying to figure out whether he was like all the other wealthy people she knew or whether he was, in fact, a normal person. Reggie had had very good reasons for distrusting the wealthy, but thankfully he'd turned out to be the latter...or so she'd thought.

Having been raised in an exclusive and snobbish Melbourne suburb, born to incredibly wealthy parents, Reggie had instantly recognised the name of Flynn Jamieson when he'd arrived at the understaffed Caribbean hospital for his six-week contract. Their fathers had been involved in some sort of business venture together and their elite community had been small, to say the least.

Of course, Flynn hadn't had a clue of her own true identity and after she'd realised he really was interested in providing medical treatment to people in need, not just working there because it had been a good opportunity to advance his career, she'd started to thaw towards him.

She'd allowed herself to be affected by his gorgeous, sexy smile, his bright, twinkling eyes, his smooth, hypnotic voice. And once she'd fallen for him, hook, line and sinker, he'd revealed his true colours, discarding her feelings and dismissing her out of hand.

And yet somehow, all these years later, he still managed to make her knees go weak with one of those smiles, make her heart pound wildly against her chest with a simple wink and make her melt in a boneless mass at the sound of his voice. It was wrong. Wrong that he still had such a hold over her emotions, and she resented him for it.

The following Monday, after she'd managed to avoid him once more during the general surgical elective theatres list, Reggie had stopped by her small office in the surgical block to finish writing up some notes and collect her computer and cellphone. It was late in the day and she was thankful the rest of the administrative staff had already left for the day because the last thing she felt like was talking to people.

'So unlike you,' she murmured, as she hunted around for her house keys, having already forgotten them twice in the past few days. She blamed Flynn's presence for her lack of joviality and general absent-mindedness and once more wished he hadn't chosen to come to

Sunshine General and inadvertently torture her just by being around.

She heard a sound outside in the corridor and instantly she was alert, listening for evidence of Flynn. Deciding to forget the search for her keys, knowing her neighbour, Melva, had the spare set, Reggie quietly locked her office door and all but sprinted out of the department.

Whether or not it had been Flynn she'd heard or one of the cleaners, she didn't care. Bumping into Flynn was too exhausting as it not only set her body into a trembling mass of uncontrollable tingles but also taxed her mind as she tried to fight the urge to throw herself into his arms and press her lips to his. She knew it was wrong to want to do that but sometimes it was difficult to deny the urge.

Reggie headed to the front of the hospital, looking forward to getting home, having a quick bite of dinner and then running a long, luxurious bath where she would soak until her skin was all wrinkled and pruney, washing away the cares of her day…and the acceptance that she was just as much attracted to Flynn as she'd ever been.

She stood at the taxi rank and looked up and down the road, unable to believe that at just after seven o'clock in the evening, on a Monday night, there were no taxis parked and waiting outside the hospital.

'There are always taxis here,' she murmured, spreading her arms wide.

'Not tonight, from the look of things,' Flynn's deep voice said from beside her, the sound causing her heart to flip-flop with delight before a ripple of awareness washed over her. Reggie closed her eyes, trying to pull some sort of shield around herself, but she'd had a busy and emotionally exhausting day and wasn't sure she had the energy for yet another run-in with Flynn.

Dragging in a deep breath, she opened her eyes and turned to look at him, deciding it was easier to face the situation than to make it worse by pretending to ignore him. 'Do you think you might not continue to creep up on me?' she asked, trying to keep her tone polite and impersonal but failing miserably.

'Only if you stop dashing from a room every time I walk in,' he countered, his clever eyes telling her he'd been aware of her avoidance tactics.

She looked down at her feet then cleared her throat. 'Er…how was Theatre this afternoon?'

Flynn stared at her for a split second before nodding. 'Good.' He paused and she noted a small smile twitching at the corners of his lips. 'No patients died.'

'Always a good thing,' she replied instantly, before she could stop herself. It was a private joke between the two of them, extending back to his first operating session in the Caribbean. The equipment at the hospital hadn't been as up to date as that in the hospitals in Australia and afterwards she'd asked him that same question.

'How did things go in Theatre, Flynn?'

'Good,' he'd replied, pulling off his cap and gown. 'No patients died.'

Reggie's laughter had filled the air at his words and it had been at that exact moment that she'd realised Flynn Jamieson was indeed a good man and she would be wrong not to give him a chance. She, herself, was proof that people shouldn't be judged by who their parents were so she shouldn't do the same to Flynn. 'Always a good thing,' she'd replied as he'd joined in with her laughter. From that day onwards, the two of them had been almost inseparable.

Reggie pushed the memory aside and glanced up and down the street as though willing a taxi to miraculously appear. She shifted her laptop bag to her other shoulder, wishing she hadn't added a few hefty manila folders filled with paperwork to it.

'You remembered,' he said softly, reaching out to take her bag from her.

'It's OK. I've got it,' she told him, grasping the strap and doing her best to ignore his comment. She didn't want to stand here and reminisce about the past.

'Of course.' He dropped his hand back to his side. 'Habit. I always used to carry your bag for you when we were together.'

'But we're not together anymore, Flynn, and I'm a big girl now and can do it all by myself.' Her polite smile was starting to slip and not only was her exhaustion shining through, so was her lack of patience. 'Look, Flynn, do you mind if we don't do the trip down memory lane? I've had a hectic day and I just want to get back to my apartment, eat and have a—'

'Relaxing soak in the tub,' he finished for her, his words indicating just how well he did know her. 'Of course you do.' He took a step away. 'I'll leave you alone.' With that, he turned and walked away without another word, leaving Reggie standing at the front of the hospital, beneath the bright lights, with other people milling around, both patients and staff.

She frowned at his quick retreat. It wasn't that Flynn was leaving her all alone, deserted in the wilderness. He was merely doing as she'd asked. She should be grateful for that, so why was it she felt guilty for sending him away?

'No taxis?' an elderly man asked as he came to stand beside her, looking up and down the street.

'There's an international sporting match being played at the stadium,' another person offered as she came to stand on the other side of Reggie.

'Ah, all the taxis have taken their chances there.' Reggie smiled and nodded, pulling her cellphone from her pocket. 'I'd best ring for one. Would you like me to book one for both of you as well?' she offered, feeling her natural joviality return. The others agreed and within minutes Reggie had ordered taxis for them. 'They said it would be about another ten minutes.'

'Thank you, dear,' the man said. 'I might go and sit down to wait.'

'I'll join you.' But no sooner were the words out of her mouth than a white car pulled up into the taxi rank. Reggie did a double take as Flynn exited the car and came round to her side, taking her bag from her shoulder and holding open the passenger door.

'Your taxi awaits, Dr Smith.'

The others who were waiting with her all laughed and clapped, drawing more attention.

'I've called for a taxi,' she spluttered as Flynn put a gentle hand beneath her elbow and guided her towards his car.

'It won't go to waste,' the elderly man said, indicating a few other people who had come to the front of the hospital, hoping to find a swag of taxis.

'So that's settled,' Flynn remarked, as a stunned Reggie sat in the passenger seat. He closed the door then turned to the other people standing there. 'I apologise for not being able to be your personal taxi but I do wish you all the merriest of Christmases and a prosperous New Year.' Then, with a small bow, he came round to the driver's side, slipped behind the wheel, buckled his seat belt and the car merged seamlessly with the flowing evening traffic.

'What…what are you doing?' she asked, the shock slowly starting to wear off.

'I'm giving you a lift home. I thought that was obvious.' Flynn snapped his fingers at her. 'Keep up, Reg.'

'Don't call me that.'

'Why not? I've always called you Reg. In fact, if memory serves me correctly, I was the only one you *allowed* to call you that.' Flynn's smile was wide and bright. 'It made me feel special.'

'That's why I want you to stop.'

'I'm not special to you anymore?'

'Flynn, can we just stop this charade?' she said abruptly, her exhausted temper getting the better of her.

'Which way do I go?'

'You go back to wherever it was you came from, get out of my life and leave me alone.'

'No. I meant to your house. I don't know where you live.'

Sighing with exasperation and deciding it was far better to work with him rather than against him as that would facilitate her arriving home sooner and thus escaping his presence, she said, 'Turn right at the next set of traffic lights. Down two blocks then right, left, right, right.'

'Right,' he said, with a small chuckle.

Reggie rolled her eyes and stared out the window, determined not to say anything else. She'd been kidnapped and she was grumpy. Why was it Flynn seemed to bring out the worst in her?

'You always used to say I brought out the best in

you,' he offered, and it was only then that Reggie realised she'd spoken out loud.

'That was before.' She shifted in her seat and stared
at him. 'I know I shouldn't aggravate the designated
driver but as you've basically kidnapped me, I just
might.' She dragged in a breath. 'What we had all those
years ago, Flynn, is over. I can learn to accept the fact
that you'll be here while Geetha's on maternity leave—'

'The next six months,' he offered.

'And I can even learn to work alongside you as a
professional colleague, but at no point in the scenario
of the two of us working at the same hospital does it
mean we're going to rekindle the relationship we had
before.' She shook her finger at him to emphasise her
words. 'You didn't choose me, Flynn. You broke off our
engagement and within less than a fortnight were married to another woman.' Reggie crossed her arms over
her chest and refused to say another word.

'Reg.' He turned right and started to slow the car.

'I told you not to call me that. I can't believe you
thought you could just waltz back into my life and be
so...so...familiar. We are not friends, Flynn. Far from
it.'

'Reg.'

'All we are is colleagues. Nothing more. There will
be no cute looks from you, no flirting, no "Do you remember when?", no—'

'Reg.' He slowed the car to a crawl, peering through
the windscreen.

'No "no patients died" type of thing. OK? We are not
a couple and we never will be,' she huffed.

'Regina! Shut. Up.' He brought the car to a stop and
pointed to the front windscreen. It was then she did

as he'd suggested and what she saw made her eyes go wide with horror.

'That's my apartment building. My building…it's on *fire!*'

Reggie opened the door and was out of the car like a shot. 'Reg! Wait!' She heard Flynn's voice in the distance but couldn't wait. Her building was on fire. Her apartment. Her neighbours' apartments. Her neighbours.

'Melva! Melva!' she called, as she ran down the street. There were police, flashing lights and people everywhere. The firefighters were doing their job, working hard to take control of the angry orange flames that were engulfing the home where she'd managed to carve out a new life for herself.

In a state of shock she continued to call out Melva's name. Her elderly neighbour would have been getting ready for bed. What if she hadn't been able to escape? What if she was still in there!

'Whoa! Reg!' Flynn was right beside her, grabbing her arms as she barrelled headlong towards the area the police had cordoned off. 'You can't go in there.'

'But she needs me.' Reggie tried to shake loose from Flynn's grasp but he was hanging onto her with a firm grip. 'Melva!' she called again.

'Stop.' A policewoman came across and stood in Reggie's path, effectively blocking her. 'That is a burning building.'

'That's *my* building,' Reggie begged. 'Please? Melva. My neighbour—' Reggie broke off as she saw a fireman coming out of the building with a woman over his shoulder. 'Melva!' She choked on the word and it was only then she felt the soothing and strong presence of Flynn right next to her, his arm around her shoulders, not only holding her back from rushing headlong into a burning building but also providing her with strength and comfort.

'We're both qualified surgeons at Sunshine General.' His words carried authority as he spoke to the police-woman. 'As the ambulances are...' he paused for a second and listened, the sirens easily heard in the distance '...still on their way, and you have a woman there who needs medical assistance, why don't you let us help out?' As he spoke, he pulled out his hospital identification, proving he wasn't lying. The policewoman checked it thoroughly and nodded.

'What about her?' She gestured towards Reggie, who was watching the fireman gently place Melva on the ground a safe distance from the burning building. His fellow firemen were already calling for his return to the building.

'Let her treat her neighbour and she'll be fine,' Flynn said.

The policewoman seemed to dither for a second but when Flynn smiled reassuringly at her she nodded. 'All right. We're already short-staffed. Medical kits are over there next to the police cars,' she said, pointing. The policewoman's partner was already kneeling by Melva's side, pressing his fingers to her carotid pulse then shaking his head.

At her words, Flynn removed his arm from Reggie's shoulders and like a racing horse bursting from the barriers Reggie was at Melva's side like a shot.

'Melva. Melva, it's Reggie. Can you hear me?'

'You know her?' the policeman asked, moving back before Reggie could shove him out of the way. Her hands were busy, checking Melva's pulse, leaning down to see if she was still breathing.

'She's my neighbour.' Now that Reggie was actually able to be doing something, she was much calmer, just as Flynn had predicted. She glanced up to find Flynn returning with the medical kit and oxygen mask, as she continued her attempts to get a response from Melva.

'You live here?'

'Lived. Past tense.' Reggie couldn't even think about everything in her apartment that was in the process of burning. All she cared about was Melva. She kept calling to her, willing her to open her eyes. Her breathing was definitely restricted. Reggie didn't like it.

'Quick. The oxygen,' she said, holding out her hands towards Flynn.

'What about your other neighbours?' the officer asked. Reggie just wanted him to keep quiet but she also knew that he had a job to do.

'The family in number two, upstairs, are interstate. The young couple in the other upstairs apartment should still be at work.' She reached into her pocket and pulled out her cellphone, tossing it at the officer and telling him the names of her neighbours. 'Search through my directory and find their information.' Reggie turned her attention to Flynn. 'Melva's pulse is faint. Her breathing is definitely restricted. We may need to intubate. No patient response.'

No sooner had the words left her lips than Melva stopped breathing.

'She's stopped,' Flynn reported. He opened the medical kit and reached for a face shield and gloves. In another instant he had checked Melva's mouth was clear and had her head tipped back, ready to perform expired air resuscitation.

'Come on, Melva. Breathe.' Reggie's words came through gritted teeth as she counted out the breaths, readying herself in position for cardiopulmonary re-suscitation. She kept counting, Flynn kept checking for a pulse.

'Come on, Melva. This is getting beyond a joke, and I'll tell you right now,' she said in time with her move-ments, 'you are not dying tonight. Not if I have anything to do with it.' Her words were clear and determined and filled with promise.

Flynn did another two breaths then checked for a pulse. 'It's there.' He looked over at Reggie, noting the look of relief cross her face.

'Atta girl, Melva.' She rested back on her heels for a second before helping Flynn to secure the oxygen mask over Melva's mouth and nose. The ambulance sirens had drawn closer and in another moment they were si-lenced, but the blue and red flashing lights filled the darkness of the night as whoever was driving came up the kerb and onto the grass, getting as close as possible to where they were treating Melva.

'I'll speak to them,' Flynn said, standing up and striding purposefully towards the paramedics.

'She has a few burns to her arms and legs,' Reggie pointed out, and reached for the medical kit. 'Melva,' she called again, still watching the rise and fall of the other woman's chest. 'We're going to take good care of you,' she said, as the paramedics came over to give them a hand. They wrapped wet towels around the burns on Melva's arms and legs, Reggie very happy when Flynn reported that her breathing was improving.

'Do you know if she has any allergies?' Flynn asked.

'Not that I know of.'

'OK.' He spoke to one of the paramedics. 'Can you get me some midazolam so we can get Melva here ready for transfer?' He returned his attention to Melva as she started to cough a little more.

Reggie quickly hooked a stethoscope into her ears and listened to Melva's breathing. 'Still rasping. Let's give her some salbutamol via nebuliser just to open those lungs.'

'Yes, Doctor,' the paramedic replied.

'Reggie?' As Melva said her name she coughed and Reggie immediately took the other woman's hand in hers.

'Yes, it's me. I'm here. You're going to be fine.'

'So much smoke. Couldn't see.' Melva's words came out broken but there was also a hint of panic in her voice and the last thing they needed right now was for Melva's anxiety to rise.

'It's OK now. Shh. I'm here. I'll take care of you.'

'But the apartments…'

'I'll take care of it. You just relax and leave everything to me.'

Flynn looked across at her. 'Reggie, if you need any help—'

'I said I'd take care of it,' Reggie returned, her words a little crisp.

'Of course.'

She frowned for a moment. Flynn? Backing down? Not insisting on being the big, strong hero, coming to the rescue of the damsel in distress? She met his gaze for a split second and saw nothing there but reassurance. Perhaps he had changed. Perhaps he was different from the way he'd been six years ago. There was truth in his eyes, as though he was desperate to let her know that he meant what he said.

Could she really trust him again? Reggie couldn't deny she was relieved he was with her, somehow empowering her with the strength and professionalism she needed to help her elderly neighbour.

Reggie pressed her fingers to Melva's pulse and was pleased to find it a little stronger than before. 'You're doing just fine, Melva.' Reggie held the other woman's hand and kissed it. 'You have an oxygen mask on so just lie still. I'm looking after you.'

'Good. Means I'll be OK.' Melva managed a weak smile beneath the mask, her eyes opening only for a second before she closed them again then started coughing.

'Relax. Breathe easy,' Reggie encouraged, and looked up to see just where Flynn was with getting that salbutamol organised. 'Flynn?' she called.

'Right here, Reg.' He was walking towards her, carrying the portable nebuliser. Soon they had Melva settled, with the salbutamol easing the pressure in her lungs as the paramedics transferred her to the stretcher.

'You'll come with me?' Melva asked, her voice still a little raspy.

'Try to keep me away,' Reggie said with a smile as Melva was settled into the ambulance. She stopped for a moment then turned and looked at their building. Smoke was billowing out but thankfully the firefighters had managed to contain the raging flames, protecting the properties on either side. People were everywhere, being kept at a distance, more police had arrived to assist with crowd control and another fire engine was just pulling up so the men and women who had already been battling the blaze for quite some time could rest and recuperate.

She knew the drill. She'd been involved in many a rescue situation over the years but now, as she continued to watch the place she'd called home become nothing more than a wreck, she couldn't help an overwhelming sense of helplessness engulf her.

Her eyes filled with tears and although she tried to blink them away, knowing she needed to remain strong, to be there for Melva, she couldn't shift them. Sniffing, she raised a shaking hand to her lips as the scene before her blurred into a watery mess. As a tear dropped from her lashes and rolled down her cheek, she almost jumped when Flynn's warm and comforting arms drew her close.

She knew she should resist. She knew she should push him away, keep her distance from the man who had broken her heart beyond repair, but she couldn't. She wanted his comfort, needed his strength, and for the first time in years Reggie gave in to the vulnerabilities she'd successfully kept at bay for far too long.

'Oh, Flynn,' she murmured against his chest, hating herself for loving the comfort he offered. 'What am I going to do now?'

'Shh,' he crooned, resting his chin on her head and tightening his hold on her. 'We'll figure it out.'

'We?' The word was barely a whisper as she snuggled in a little closer to him, her ear pressed to his chest, and there she could hear that his heart was beating a lot faster than it should. 'We?' she asked again, a little louder, and as she edged back just a touch, lifting her head so she could look at his face, she saw in his eyes determination mixed with a healthy dose of repressed desire.

'We,' he confirmed with a definitive nod.

CHAPTER THREE

'REGGIE?'

She felt a hand on her shoulder rousing her from her light doze. Someone was gently shaking her awake, their deep voice tender and soothing.

'Reg?'

She breathed in deeply, recognising the sound of Flynn's voice. Oh, Flynn. How she'd missed him. The way he'd always held her close, supporting her, listening to her, comforting her. She'd loved the way he'd called her 'Reg', the one syllable sounding so special and unique and perfect from his lips. She sighed with happiness, letting the dream of his presence wash over her.

She remembered the first time he'd kissed her, *really* kissed her, not just a quick peck on the cheek. She'd all but melted into his arms and kissed him back with equal abandonment. Until that moment she'd never known kissing someone could feel so real, so right, so romantic.

They'd known each other for only two weeks and she'd been astounded at how his thoughts had been so aligned with hers. 'I just knew it would be perfect between us,' he'd whispered against her mouth when they'd finally come up for air. As though by unspoken mutual consent, from that moment onwards they'd been a couple. They'd strolled hand in hand along the beach at sunset, worked side by side at the hospital, gazed longingly into each other's eyes. She had accepted his words, his touch, his love, and she'd thought it would last forever.

Sadness crept into her soul and she started to rouse from the dream, wishing she had the chance to go back and rewrite her past. Oh, Flynn. Why? Why? She shifted, trying to shake off the tender hand on her shoulder…the one that was trying to wake her.

'Reg?' She heard his voice, more clearly now. She felt his breath fan her face and slowly her mind lifted itself from the fuzziness of that state between dreams and reality. Reggie opened her eyes and looked around, taking a moment to remember exactly where she was.

She was in the female ward, sitting in a chair by Melva's bedside. She'd obviously fallen asleep, the exhaustion of the day having finally caught up with her. A busy day at the hospital and then…and then the fire. The fire that had burned her apartment and all her belongings to the ground and had almost taken Melva's life. She looked at Flynn, realising he was crouched down beside her chair, his lips curved in a small smile.

'Hi, there.'

'Was I snoring?' she asked, and was delighted when his smile increased.

'Not that I can report. I'll have to check with Ayana, though,' he said, indicating where the night sister was seated at the nurses' station, writing up some paperwork.

Reggie looked back at Melva, pleased to see her friend sleeping soundly. The echo-cardiograph was still monitoring Melva's heart rate and from what Reggie could see, everything looked to be within normal parameters.

'She's doing well,' Flynn confirmed, and stood when Reggie eased herself out of the chair, wanting to read Melva's latest set of observations. Feeling stiff from sitting too long, Reggie stretched her arms up over her head, shifting slightly from side to side as she worked out the kinks in her back. As she lowered her arms she glanced at Flynn, surprised to find him watching her every move. She blushed and straightened the hem of her knit top, which had ridden up a little.

'Er...' She cleared her throat as she tried to focus on the information on the monitor. Come on, Reggie. Pull yourself together. It's not as though Flynn hasn't admired your body before. Good heavens, she used to go swimming with him in the sea wearing a bikini. But that had been then, when they'd been together as a couple. This was now, when he was nothing more than a colleague...and possibly a friend?

He had stated he was going to help her out and he'd held her so tenderly, so carefully, so...lovingly? She pushed the thought away and gave her thoughts a mental shake.

'All her vitals are steady,' Flynn continued. 'Her heart is strong, the burns on her arms and legs are bandaged and will eventually heal,' he continued.

'And on top of all this she now has the emotional trauma of dealing with losing her life-long possessions, reminders of her husband and family and all those trinkets she's collected over the years. She shouldn't be forced to start again, not at her age.' Reggie reached for Melva's hand and held it in hers. 'She has been such a good friend to me since I moved into the apartment block. I need to do whatever I can for her...and for the other tenants.'

'The fire wasn't your fault, Reggie,' he pointed out.

'Preliminary findings show there was a fault with the wiring.'

'Then I should have been more diligent, forcing the landlord to check these things out more thoroughly.' She pressed a kiss to Melva's hand before she turned and walked to the end of the bed. 'I feel as though I've failed her. What sort of Christmas is she supposed to have now?'

Flynn put both hands on her shoulders then turned her to face him. When she didn't immediately look at him he placed his fingers gently beneath her chin and lifted it so their gazes could meet. 'It's not your fault.' His words were earnest and intent.

'But—'

'It's not your fault.' He spoke with carefulness, as though he was desperate to get the words to sink in.

'Still, there has to have been something I could have done to prev—'

He silenced her by pressing his index finger tenderly to her lips, knowing the touch would effectively silence her. He leaned in closer, bringing his mouth closer to her ear so she could hear him when he whispered clearly, *It's not your fault.* Then he gathered her into his arms and held her tightly. 'You're not going to do yourself any favours by playing the what-if game, Reg.'

She closed her eyes as his message finally began to penetrate through her thick skull. 'I know you want to rewind time, to do anything you can to spare Melva the emotional upheaval she's going to go through, but you can't.' His words were barely above a whisper as she once more allowed herself to rest within his arms.

How she'd missed this. Having someone with big strong arms hold her, comfort her, support her in times of need. How she'd missed Flynn. She felt so comfortable and secure in his arms that a moment later, she yawned, a big, long yawn.

'You're exhausted,' she heard him murmur, but now that she'd mentally accepted there was nothing she could have done to alter tonight's outcome of the fire, it was as though her entire body was starting to shut down.

Plus, Flynn was making it very comfortable for her to stand there, leaning into him, knowing his big, strong arms would support her and keep her safe. At this particular moment it didn't matter one jot what had happened between them all those years ago. What mattered was that Flynn was offering comfort and she was going to be selfish and accept it.

The memories from her past, the memories she'd tried so hard to push away, to ignore, to never think about again, were returning with a vengeance as she continued to lean against him. She knew he wouldn't let her fall, that he would support her, and for a wild moment she desperately wanted to go back in time. Back to when Flynn had professed his love for her. Back to a moment when her life, for the very first time, had felt...complete.

'Go back,' she mumbled into his chest, her words incoherent.

'Reggie?' Flynn eased away just slightly to look down at her, but she only seemed to snuggle in closer. Who was he to argue? He closed his eyes, allowing himself to absorb the sensation of once again having his Reg in his arms. It was clear the attraction they'd felt for each other all those years ago was still alive and well...at least, it was on his side. Could she feel it, too?

'Reggie?' He tried again and when the only answer he received was her steady and even breathing, he realised that the day had definitely taken its toll on her. Not only had she been watching over Melva for the past few hours but she'd also answered a barrage of questions from the police, providing them with whatever information she could. Thankfully, both her other neighbours had been contacted and although they were devastated at the loss of their belongings, at least none of them had lost their lives. Therefore, he wasn't the least bit surprised at Reggie being so completely wiped out that she was literally asleep on her feet.

'Come on, Reg,' he murmured, shifting her slightly in his arms so he could guide her as they walked quietly out of the ward.

'Where are we going?' she asked, half roused. He couldn't help but smile down at the gorgeous sight of her, her short, black hair sticking out a little at the sides and her eyelids half-closed.

'You need sleep,' he replied.

'Good idea. Residential wing will have a bed free.'

'Goodnight, Ayana,' Flynn called quietly as he waved to the night nurse. 'If there's any change in Melva's condition—'

'I'll call you and Reggie immediately,' Ayana promised. 'Get her to a bed, and soon, Flynn. She really is asleep on her feet, isn't she?' Ayana smiled as Reggie continued to lean against Flynn. It would be far easier for him to scoop her into his arms and carry her through the hospital but he was already mindful of the looks they were receiving with her snuggled so closely against him. The last thing he wanted was for Reggie to have to deal with a barrage of gossip on top of everything else that had happened to her.

They headed out of the ward towards the lift, Reggie more than content to let him guide her. That way

she didn't have to think about anything. She couldn't
remember being this exhausted since she'd been an in-
tern, trying to cope with the all-nighters followed by a
full day shift. Perhaps the trauma of losing all her possessions, of the impending frustration and stress of dealing with the insurance company, of having to go out in
the morning and buy new clothes and shoes and... She
didn't even own a toothbrush. Not anymore.

'And all the Christmas presents,' she groaned, her
words muffled as she spoke into Flynn's chest, another
layer of stress falling on her shoulders.

'What?' Flynn bent his head so he could hear her
more clearly.

'I'd finished my Christmas shopping. Now it's all
gone.' She wanted to cry, she wanted to scream and bellyache and wail, but she was just too exhausted.

'We'll sort it out,' Flynn promised her as they headed
out into the humid December night.

'Thank you, Flynn. You always were so reliable...
except, you know, when you broke my heart.'

'You're mumbling, Reg. Can't understand a word,'
he told her. 'And you're starting to trip over your own
feet,' she heard him say, and the next instant she felt
as light as a feather, floating along in the breeze. She
looped her arms around Flynn's neck and rested her
head against his shoulder, only belatedly realising he'd
scooped her off her feet and was carrying her, striding
purposefully towards the residential wing like the gal-
lant hero she'd always thought him to be.

'Flynn,' she sighed as her head was finally placed
onto a soft pillow. She had no idea just how much time
had passed and could have sworn she'd been strapped
into a car at one point. Perhaps Flynn had decided to

drive around to the residential wing rather than carry her the entire way.

At any rate, she was simply glad to finally be in a bed, a sheet being pulled over her, the ceiling fan whirring gently above to keep her cool throughout the night. Someone was removing her shoes and once that was done she drew her knees up and snuggled into the inviting world of dreams.

'Sleep sweet, Reg.'

Flynn's glorious deep words washed over her and then she dreamed he'd placed a kiss on her forehead. 'Mmm, Flynn. I've missed you,' she whispered.

He straightened up and stared down at the woman sleeping in his spare room. She'd missed him? Really? Was that just the exhaustion talking? Did she mean 'miss' as in she'd wanted to see him again? Because from the moment he'd seen her at the hospital the impression he'd gained had definitely been the opposite, especially as she'd spent the better part of the last week avoiding him.

With her breathing settling into an even rhythm, letting him know she was definitely sound asleep, Flynn knew he should leave yet he couldn't seem to move. Watching Reggie sleep made his heart contract with pain and pleasure as his mind was flooded with a round of what-if's.

She was the woman he'd once loved with all his heart, the woman he'd planned to marry and spend the rest of his life with, the woman who had managed to show him he was a person of worth, to accept him for exactly who he was…and then everything had exploded. He'd been weak, had allowed himself to be manipulated, and it had brought him nothing but pain and mortification.

'Not anymore.' He shook his head and exhaled heavily. When he'd accepted the job at Sunshine General, he hadn't known Reggie was working there, not until a few days before his starting date, when he'd had a meeting with Geetha to fill in the remaining paperwork.

'The staff here are very friendly, especially Reggie,' Geetha had told him after they'd finished dealing with the red tape. Flynn had literally frozen at the name.

'Reggie?' It might not be the same person, he'd rationalised, astonished to find his heartbeat had increased. The name 'Reggie' might actually be referring to a man named Reginald, not a dynamic woman called Regina who had the biggest blue eyes, fringed with dark lashes and the most encompassing laugh he'd ever heard.

'Reggie Smith, she's one of our general surgeons.' Geetha had shaken her head. 'Incredibly talented, should have been head of department years ago but instead she prefers to work as a functioning member of the team, at least that's what she tells me.'

'Reggie Smith.' Flynn had settled back in his chair, his heart racing at the thought that soon he'd see Reggie again. Was that a good thing? He'd thought about her constantly over the past six years, especially when his marriage had broken up. He'd been tempted time and time again to find her, to track her down, but what would he say to her when they met again? *I'm sorry I broke your heart. Can we try again, please, because I can't seem to get you out of my mind?*

He'd also presumed she would be happily married with a couple of children, that she'd moved on with her life…her life without him. Thoughts like that had stopped him from trying to find her. Reggie deserved the world of happiness, especially after the abominable way he'd treated her, and if she'd found that happiness with some other man, he did not want to know about it.

Now, though, not only had he been granted the opportunity to see her but to also work alongside her. She wasn't married, didn't have children, and if the way she'd just whispered his name into the pillow was any indication, perhaps there was a small spark of hope. It was clear, on his part, that the attraction he'd felt all those years ago certainly hadn't diminished. The question was, could Reggie forgive him for his past behaviour? If she couldn't, there was no hope of them moving forward together.

His phone started to ring and he quickly left the room, wondering who would be calling him at this hour of the night. Another emergency? He hoped not. He didn't want to leave Reggie alone in his town house, concerned she'd wake up and not know where she was.

He checked the caller ID and saw it was Violet. He quickly answered the call. 'Hey, Vi. Everything OK?'

'It's Ian,' she told him. 'He has a temperature. I don't know what to do. You know I fall to pieces when he gets sick.'

'What are his symptoms?' Flynn walked through to the lounge and slumped down into a comfortable chair as he listened to Violet describe five-year-old Ian's symptoms. 'It does sound like it's just a tummy bug, especially as you haven't been feeling well. You've given him paracetamol?'

'No. No. Good idea. I'll do that. Hold on. Don't hang up.'

Flynn closed his eyes, feeling strange receiving a phone call from Violet while Reggie was asleep in the next room. It was as though the two different parts of his life, family and the separate life he was trying to build, were once more colliding. He'd been given a second chance with Reggie and he wasn't going to blow this one. If she knew he was still in contact with Violet, that might jeopardise everything, and the fact that she'd just been murmuring his name in her sleep was a good sign that things *were* progressing the way he was hoping.

However, he also knew he'd have to tell her about Violet...at some point. Right now, though, he was going to do his best to keep his two very different worlds as far apart as possible. He didn't want anything jeopardising the chance that he and Reggie might be able to pick up where they'd left off six years ago. Now, that certainly would be something to dream about.

Reggie opened her eyes, stretching her arms above her head. She'd had a wonderful sleep but a moment later, as her mind began to wake up, she remembered the events of yesterday evening. Her apartment had burned down.

'Melva!' She sat bolt upright in the bed, thinking fast. She'd get out of bed and go check on Melva, then start figuring out what to do next. No doubt she'd have to go shopping as the clothes on her back were literally the only clothes she had. She could borrow some from Mackenzie and...

She frowned, looking around the room, taking in her surroundings. This wasn't a tiny room in the residential wing. 'Where am I?' As she continued to inspect the room, she realised she was in Sunainah's spare room... or what had previously been Sunainah's spare room. Her friend had moved out of this town house when she'd married Elliot. The town house had been vacant since then and listed on the hospital's bulletin board. Her eyes widened as realisation dawned. 'Oh, no!'

Reggie flicked back the covers and checked the floor for her shoes, quickly slipping her feet into them as she tried to piece together what she could remember of last night's events *after* the fire.

She'd been at Melva's bedside. Sunainah, Macken-zie and Bergan had all come to find her once they'd heard the news—her friends were always there when she needed their support. Then, being the stubborn woman she was, she'd refused to leave Melva's side until her neighbour had been settled in the ward. She could remember sitting by Melva's bed…then…she'd fallen asleep. Someone had woken her up and—

'Flynn!'

Reggie shot to her feet and opened the spare-room door, pushing her hands through her hair as she walked through the lower part of the town house towards the kitchen—Flynn's kitchen. She was in Flynn Jamieson's town house and by the scents of coffee and pancakes wafting from the kitchen it appeared he was making breakfast.

Sure enough, she found him standing at the stove, expertly flipping pancakes in the air and catching them in the frying pan. 'Flynn?'

'Ah.' He turned and looked at her over his shoulder, his smile bright and welcoming. 'Good morning, Reggie.' He indicated the table, which was set with plates, knives and forks, a glass of juice and a bottle of maple syrup in the middle. 'Take a seat and I'll bring you your breakfast.'

'You know how to cook now?' Still trying to wrap her head around this surreal moment, of having Flynn cook breakfast for her, she moved towards the table and dropped down into the chair, glad of its support. 'Back in the Caribbean you weren't sure how to boil water.'

He grinned at her. 'I wasn't *that* bad but, yes, during my time there I realised a lot of things about myself and how I needed to become more self-sufficient.' He checked the pancake again. 'Almost done.'

'You always were full of surprises,' Reggie murmured, her tone indicating that some of those 'surprises' hadn't always been good ones.

Flynn's answer was to wink at her, and her insides instantly flooded with a tingling warmth. Why, oh, why couldn't she be immune to his charm? She immediately looked away from him and stared at the empty plate in front of her, trying to get her thought processes jump-started.

'I've called the hospital,' Flynn said a moment later, 'and been informed that Melva has slept peacefully throughout the night and was sitting up, drinking a cup of tea.'

Reggie lifted her head and sighed with relief. 'That's great news. Thanks for the update.'

'You're welcome. Coffee?'

'Uh...most definitely, please.' She frowned as she watched him pour her a cup of coffee, not adding any milk or sugar before placing it on the table before her.

'You still take it black, right? No sugar?'

'Correct.'

'That's because you're sweet enough.' He smiled brightly. 'Isn't that what you always used to say?'

'Flynn, stop it.'

'Stop what?'

'Trying to take us down memory lane.' She spread her arms wide. 'What are you doing here?'

He stared at her as though she'd gone completely loopy. 'Did you hit your head last night? Are you feeling all right?'

'Flynn,' she growled, her teeth gritted, her tone filled with warning. He had the audacity to laugh.

'Reg, I'm not exactly sure what you mean.'

'Here. In *this* particular town house.'

'It was listed on the bulletin—'

'I know. I know it was listed but why did *you*, of all people, have to move in?'

'I don't follow.'

'Sunainah used to live here and Richard lived here before her and before that Richard's parents and before that…I don't have a clue, but the point is, you're living slap bang in the middle of my three closest friends.'

'And the problem with that is…?' he asked, carrying the frying pan towards her and placing a perfectly round, perfectly cooked pancake onto her plate.

'Thank you,' she said politely. 'It's just odd that *you*, the man I was once going to marry, is living *here*. Among my friends. In the town house they wanted me to move into. Joining the cul-de-sac crew.'

'There's a crew?' His eyes were alive with delight at this news. 'Do they get together for movie nights and dinners?'

'Flynn, be serious.'

'I am. Do you know how much I've always wanted to be accepted as just part of a crew, part of a team?'

That stopped her. 'You have?' She was surprised at his words and stared at him for a moment, realising there was still so much she didn't know about him.

'Anyway, you were saying your friends wanted you to move in here?'

'Yes, but I was more than happy where I…was.' Reggie sighed as the weight of the previous evening's events fell on her shoulders like a tonne of bricks. She slumped forward and buried her head in her hands, not even the delicious scent of the pancakes able to help in this situation.

Flynn put the frying pan back on the stove top, adding more mixture before coming over, placing his hands on her shoulders and gently starting to massage them. 'I'm sorry your place burnt down, Reg.' His words were simple, effective, perfect.

'So am I,' she said, leaning back a little to grant him more access to her neck, her eyes closing at the touch of his hands. How did he still manage to know exactly what she needed? Straightforward words and a bit of support. No flowery sentiments, no immediate solutions to problems. Just support. That was all she needed at this moment and he was offering it in a caring and gentle manner.

'You still have magic hands,' she sighed after a few minutes. 'And thank you for the pancakes. They're my favourite.'

'I remember.'

'They do make me happy, Flynn, I just can't...'

'You can't show it the way you usually do. The ever optimistic, happy and bubbly Reggie. I get it.'

'Get what?'

'With me, everything's different. You think there's too much water under the bridge between us. That it would be impossible for things to move forward between us.' He nodded. 'I understand.'

'Do you?' Did he really understand just how much he'd hurt her all those years ago?

'I might even be so bold as to declare that I understand *you*, Reggie.'

She laughed without humour. 'I've changed.' She shifted a little in her chair, acutely aware of the way he was making her feel with his hands on her shoulders, massaging gently. The air between them seemed to be charged with unspoken conversations, things they should have said but hadn't…things they shouldn't have said but had.

'Everyone changes, Reg, but hopefully not in essentials,' he offered, releasing her shoulders. 'I think you're still the same Reggie, wanting to help others, smiling, laughing, spreading sunshine wherever possible. I watched you do that when we were together in Sint Maarten, amazed and in awe of your ability and—' He dropped his hands and quickly pulled out the chair next to her and sat down, facing her, his expression determined. 'I'd like to help, Reggie. I'd like to take a leaf out of your book and spread a little sunshine.'

'Wha—? Flynn?' She closed her eyes and shook her head for a moment. 'I don't understand.'

'I want to help you and your friends. I can help by relocating Melva and your other neighbours.' His words were intense and earnest. 'And…' he held up a hand '…before you say I'm doing what all wealthy people do and throwing money at the problem, I want you to know that's not entirely true. My intentions are pure and honourable. Even if these people weren't your friends, even if they were complete strangers, if I'd heard about their hardship, I would still have wanted to help.'

Reggie thought on his words for a moment, seeing the truth in his eyes. He seemed so completely animated at the idea, his eyes twinkling with anticipatory delight. She wished he wouldn't look at her that way because right now he was far too handsome for his own good and that simply made it all the more difficult for her to keep her distance. Besides, who was she to stop him from helping others? 'I think that would be a nice thing to do, Flynn. Thank you.'

'So you'll accept my help?'

'Yes. I think my neighbours and I would be very grateful for your help, especially if you can help with relocation. Trying to find a new place to live this close to Christmas? It really *would* take a Christmas miracle to pull it off.'

'Then be prepared for a miracle.' He stood and returned to the stove, expertly flipping the pancake. 'Because I already have a plan with regard to temporary accommodation for you and your neighbours.'

'You do?'

'Yes. I've had a look online and there's a small apartment complex, near shops and public transport, with three partially furnished vacant apartments.'

'Three?'

'Yes. One for Melva, once she's ready to leave hospital, and the other two for your other neighbours.'

'What about me?' she asked, her tone a little indignant.

'Ah. Now, for you I have the perfect place. It's not going to be too far from Melva and the others, it's close to the hospital, it's furnished and the landlord has said you can move in today.'

'Today? It sounds like a miracle. Where is this place?'

Flynn winked at her and spread his arms wide. 'It's here. You're going to live with me!'

CHAPTER FOUR

'Whʌt?'

Reggie stared at him as though he'd grown another head but Flynn either didn't notice or didn't care. '*Live...* with you?' Her heart was pounding wildly in her chest at the mere thought of living with Flynn, of sharing the same intimate space as him, of seeing him last thing at night and first thing in the morning. She was glad she was sitting down as her entire body had turned into a trembling mass of jelly.

'Why not? It makes perfect sense. I have a spare room and you'll have sole use of the bathroom. I can use the *en suite* and we work at the same hospital.' He shrugged one shoulder. 'It makes perfect sense.'

'And you're sure this other place you've found only has three free apartments?'

He smiled and nodded as though humouring an indulgent child. 'Yes, Reg.'

Could he hear the hysteria in her voice, see the panic in her eyes? She was positive he could from the way he was still trying to sell her on the idea. 'So what do you say, new roomie? Let's start the day with a healthy...' he stopped and looked down at the pancakes '...or sort of healthy breakfast.'

Reggie continued to gape at him, her mouth hanging

open as he plated up his pancake and carried it to the table. Before he sat down, he removed bowls of fresh strawberries and whipped cream from the fridge, placing them on the table next to the maple syrup. As far as he was concerned, this was a done deal. She had no say in it and anger started to replace her earlier incredulity.

'I am not moving in here.' She enunciated each word crisply.

He considered her words for a moment then asked logically, 'So where will you go?' He added strawberries, cream and syrup to his pancake, behaving as though this was just another ordinary breakfast conversation.

'I'll go to a hotel for a while.'

'And waste your money when there's a perfectly good room—free of charge—here for you? Until the insurance money comes in, you're better off using your funds to buy clothes and shampoo and other essentials you'll need, rather than having to pay for accommodation.' His words were matter-of-fact and logical and she hated him for them.

She sighed again, her frustration clear. Didn't he realise that with what had happened between them, with the way he'd taken her to the highest of highs when he'd confessed his love and proposed to her then plummeted her to the lowest of lows less than twenty-four hours later when he'd broken her heart by cancelling their engagement, that there was no way she could move in with him?

'Mmm, smells good.' He pointed to her plate. 'Come on, Reg. Eat up. We're due at the hospital in an hour's time.'

'What?' She blinked at him in astonishment. 'You're not even going to suggest I take the day off? That given the circumstances of my recent emotional trauma, of losing practically everything I own, except for my laptop, my phone and the clothes on my back, I shouldn't stay in bed and rest?'

'I know you, remember.' He leaned over and spooned some strawberries onto her pancake. 'Regardless of what may or may not be happening in your life, the last thing you would ever do is let your patients down. You're not about to cancel a fully booked outpatient clinic because of personal reasons. You and I both know that being with your patients, helping them out and making their lives just that little bit easier, is going to be the best medicine to take your mind off things…at least, for a little while.'

She frowned at him. He did know her, at least on some levels. On other levels…she'd kept a lot hidden from him, previously rationalising that they had a lifetime together to discover all there was to know about each other.

'True. Working will help me to process everything that's happened,' she rationalised, including Flynn's offer for her to stay with him. 'Working will keep my mind focused.' She would go to work, see her patients, help people out, spread a little sunshine, as Flynn had termed it, and then, she was sure, life would seem a little clearer. At least, so she hoped. She looked down at her pancakes and breathed in appreciatively. 'These do smell good.'

'They taste good, too.' He ate another mouthful and winked at her, the action causing Reggie's insides to start fluttering. Why was it that one simple look from him, whether it was a wink or a smile or one of his long stares across a crowded room, made her feel so… special, so unique, so feminine? Flynn had always had been able to turn her insides to mush, to make her want to fan her face because her cheeks were tinged with heat from excited embarrassment. Now was no exception and it was far easier to concentrate on eating than trying to avoid his hypnotic gaze.

She really had no intention of permanently staying here with him because even the thought of living under the same roof as Flynn set her entire body on fire. The man was too dangerous at the best of times but to be around him both at work and at home, no doubt dreaming about him whilst she slept, would make it nigh on impossible for her to keep her emotions in check.

Still, his offer did solve her immediate problem so for the moment she would just let everything roll. She would have breakfast and a shower, mentally and figuratively washing the grime of yesterday away before popping over to Mackenzie's to borrow some clean clothes. She was glad he'd mentioned that he'd use the en suite because even thinking about standing naked beneath Flynn's shower, with him in the same house, made her feel all flushed with self-consciousness. Perhaps it would be better to just go to Mackenzie's and shower there.

After eating half of her pancake and enjoying her coffee, she was about to tell him of her plans when he beat her to it.

'I need to dash to the shops before we head to the hospital so why don't you make free use of the place? Wash away all the bad things that happened yesterday and reconnect with your usual optimistic self?' He smiled encouragingly as he said the words. 'Oh, and I contacted Mackenzie last night and she's brought over some clothes for you. They're in the drawers and the cupboard in the spare room—or *your* room as it now is.'

'You…contacted Macken—' She stopped and shook her head, unable to believe how thoughtful he'd been. 'It would have been very late.'

'Your friends love you, Reg.' He spoke softly and with sincerity. 'They don't care what time of day or night it is, they're there for you. That type of friendship is rare and incredibly special.' He looked down at his plate for a moment before meeting her gaze once more. 'Only a fool would throw away such a thing.'

His words were slightly pointed and she wondered whether he was calling himself a fool. Was he admitting that he'd made a mistake all those years ago? Was he saying he wanted to reinstate himself into her friendship circle? Was he a friend who…loved her?

Reggie found it difficult to look away. There, seated opposite her, was the man who had always been in perfect control. He'd been immaculately groomed and dressed from the first day they'd met in Sint Maarten. Being raised in a wealthy, controlled environment where most decisions had been pre-set for him had been something he hadn't even thought of rebelling against until he'd met her. He'd told her she'd liberated him, shown him a different side to life, and that his love was hers forever. And she'd stupidly believed him. She should be wary not to make the same mistakes twice.

She tried to swallow but found her throat exceedingly dry. Reaching for her orange juice, she was surprised to find her hand trembling a little. Still, drinking the cool, refreshing liquid helped to break the intense moment.

'Had enough?' he asked, pointing to her plate and breaking the moment. She nodded quickly, not trusting her voice to work. Flynn stood and quickly cleared the table. She watched him for a few minutes as he moved comfortably around the kitchen. He had such swift and defined movements, those broad shoulders of his looking firm and in control, the material from his crisp, white shirt pulling tautly across his triceps.

Reggie breathed out slowly, her gaze hungrily taking in every nuance of the man. She swallowed and cleared her throat, and when he looked her way, she realised she quickly looked away. 'Er...' She racked her sluggish mind for something to say. 'Breakfast was delicious. Whoever taught you to cook did a good job.'

'That would have been my cooking teacher at the community centre.' His tone dipped a little as he spoke, his eyebrows raised in silent question, his eyes letting her know he'd been well aware of her visual caresses.

Reggie frowned and looked away. 'Not your wife?'

'My ex-wife,' he replied pointedly, then shook his head. 'She had no idea how to cook either. One of my patients put me onto the class and the next thing I knew I was learning how to make a beef Wellington.'

'You can do a beef Wellington? I can't even do that.'

He grinned. 'Then I shall have to make you one.' He gave the countertops a final wipe. 'Perhaps there are quite a few things you don't realise about me.' Like how he was determined to show her he'd changed, that he was willing to make amends for the way he'd treated her all those years ago, like how he was almost desperate for her forgiveness.

'Perhaps,' she said, surprised at the huskiness in her voice. What was it about this man that set her alight so instantly? They'd met, they'd worked together, they'd tried to fight the natural attraction that had sprung up between them but had failed. Flynn had confessed that perhaps it was a good thing, perhaps the mutual chemistry they felt for each other was one of those rare gifts that shouldn't be ignored, so they hadn't bothered to try ignoring it at all and thus had begun the happiest, most wonderful weeks of Reggie's life. Flynn holding her. Flynn laughing with her. Flynn kissing her.

Six weeks. They'd known each other for just six weeks. Friendly colleagues for two weeks, dating for two more and then falling in love for two blissful weeks. So fast, so quick, so incredibly perfect.

As he stared back at her from the other side of the kitchen, she really felt powerless to look away, as though the past and the present were colliding and both of them could sense it. When her cellphone rang, she almost jumped out of her skin. Flynn chuckled before reaching across to the bench where he'd obviously put it last night. He'd even plugged it in to recharge the battery. How thoughtful. She frowned for a moment. Had he been this thoughtful six years ago?

'Mackenzie,' he remarked, looking at the picture of her friend that had come up on the display.

'Oh…uh…thanks.' Reggie rose from her chair and accepted the phone, taking it into the spare room so she could have some privacy. 'Mackenzie?'

'How are you doing this morning?'

'I'm at Flynn's place!' She leaned back against the door, ensuring it was closed. 'I must have been so tired he brought me home with him and put me to bed!' Her words were half whispered, half squeaked as she spoke at the speed of light.

'I know.' Mackenzie chuckled.

'Oh, of course you do. You came over and helped him by delivering some clothes! Why didn't you wake me up?'

'Not on your life, Reggie. You needed sleep.' Mackenzie said in her best motherly voice. 'Flynn sent me,

Bergan and Sunainah a text message telling us you were staying with him. I think it's a great idea.'

'But he doesn't just want me to stay for last night, he wants me to *move in with him*.'

'I know.'

'Do you know everything? Does everyone else know what's going on in my life except me?'

'It's not like that, Reggie.'

'And I'll bet you all think this is a good idea? Are you insane? This is *Flynn* we're talking about. The man who broke my heart into tiny little pieces and scattered them to the wind.'

'I remember.'

'I cried on your shoulder, I ate too much ice cream, I went over and over everything he'd ever said to me, trying to figure out what I'd done wrong to chase him away.'

'I remember.'

'I talked about him ad nauseam, I drove you insane. I told you time and time again that I was over him but I was just kidding myself and then, when I finally *did* get over him and moved on with my life, he swaggers back in and *takes over*.'

'He's not taking over. He's only trying to be nice and helpful, especially as since it's Christmas the majority of hotels are already booked up. Add to that the fact that Bergan doesn't have room because Richard's parents are coming home for Christmas, Sunainah's place is full because she married into a ready-made family and I have one of John's sisters and her family arriving the day after tomorrow.'

Reggie slid down the door, crumpling into a heap on the carpet, realising the truth of what Mackenzie was saying. 'I'd forgotten all that.'

'Not surprising. Look, honey, I'm not trying to make light of you losing everything in the fire, it's completely devastating and it will take a while for you to process things, both with the mounds of insurance paperwork and on an emotional level, but staying at Flynn's keeps you close to us, to *your* family, and right now you need to be surrounded by family. We're all here for you and we'll do whatever we can to help—and so will Flynn,' she added. 'He's a good guy, Reggie, and no matter what happened between the two of you all those years ago, you know, deep down inside, that it's true.'

'It's not a question of whether he's good or not, Mackenzie, it's a question of whether or not I can resist him,' Reggie blurted.

'Oh.' Mackenzie said the word slowly as though realisation was just dawning. 'Ah. Yes. I hadn't thought of things from that angle, just the logistics of your present predicament.'

'Well, start thinking that way. I can't stay here with Flynn. I can't stop staring at him, remembering how it felt to be held by him, to be kissed by him, to be in love with him.' She closed her eyes, the pain from her past beginning to return. 'He hurt me, Mackenzie, and, yes, it's all in the past, but what if I allow myself to get close to him and he hurts me *again*?'

'What if he doesn't? Reggie, the one thing I remember you telling me a few years after you'd broken up was that you thought Flynn had never really opened up to you, that the attraction between you two had happened so fast—'

'And the break-up even faster,' Reggie put in.

'That at times you wondered if you ever really knew him. Plus,' Mackenzie continued before Reggie could say another word, 'there was also a lot about your past that you never told him.'

Reggie opened her eyes and looked at the blank mushroom-coloured wall opposite her. 'True.'

'Maybe this is the chance to rectify that.'

'What point is there in opening up to him now? Rehashing the wounds of my past?'

'Call it finishing unfinished business. You always wondered how Flynn would react once he learned who you really were. Now is your chance. Who knows? It might be cathartic. Once he knows the truth of your past, if he reacts the way you always thought he would—'

'By rejecting me, like everyone else from that world,' she interrupted again.

'Then it might help you get him out of your system once and for all. Then you can really move forward with your life.'

'I have moved forward,' Reggie declared, not wanting to open the box she'd hidden in the back of her mind, the one she'd marked 'Do Not Open'. 'I've changed a lot. I'm happier than I used to be. I've put myself out there. I've dated other men and—'

'And secretly used Flynn as your yardstick the entire time. No man was ever good enough. Or, on the flip side, you'd end up solving your date's problems and helping them get back together with their old girlfriends.' It was Mackenzie's turn to interrupt. 'Think about it, Reggie. You and Flynn have unfinished business. Talk to him. You might be surprised at what you discover.'

Reggie pondered Mackenzie's words for a moment, realising there was a hint of common sense in them. 'I didn't know he could cook and those pancakes were delicious.'

'There you go, then. Plus, if you think about it, with the way Christmas tends to get hectic in surgical theatres, you'll probably be spending most of your time at the hospital, rather than catching up on sleep at Flynn's place.'

'It does get busy.'

'Then after Christmas you'll have plenty of time to look around and find somewhere to live that suits your needs, and once the insurance money comes in, I'll gladly volunteer to go furniture shopping with you.'

'Yeah.' Reggie sat up a little straighter, her confidence beginning to return. 'I don't need to stay here forever, just the next few weeks.' She thought it through rationally. 'And I do spend a lot of time at the hospital over Christmas. I really wouldn't be here all that much.'

'See?'

'And it was very nice of him to offer.'

'He's a nice man and, if you let yourself admit it, I think you'll see he's also a good friend.'

'Friend?' She tilted her head to the side and considered the word. 'I guess I've never really thought about Flynn that way, as a friend. It was so powerful and intense between us we didn't really have the opportunity to truly become friends.'

'So you'll stay?'

'You know…' Reggie levered herself up off the floor '…I think I will.'

'Yay! A temporary member of the cul-de-sac crew.'

Reggie laughed at Mackenzie's words, feeling a return of her usual optimistic self. 'I can already hear your thoughts, Kenz. Dinner parties, games nights and Christmas parties.'

'You know me too well, Reggie.' Mackenzie laughed along with her friend. 'Feel better?'

'I do. I really do, which, given I've lost practically everything, is not a bad feeling to be having.'

'Good. Oh. I've gotta go. Ruthie's just woken up.'

'Right-oh. I'll talk to you later.'

'You know it, cul-de-sac crew member!'

Reggie was still smiling as she entered the bathroom, finding a set of towels waiting there for her along with a fresh bar of soap. 'How thoughtful.' And he really was, she realised. Taking care of her last night, making her breakfast this morning and offering to help relocate her neighbours. 'Friends,' she repeated to herself as she stepped beneath the soothing spray of the shower. 'I can be friends with Flynn.' She was proud of the conviction in her words.

By the time he returned from wherever he'd had to go, Reggie was showered and dressed in the borrowed clothes.

'Wow.' Flynn's eyebrows shot up as he saw her standing there dressed in a navy skirt, white shirt and navy jacket. Her short feathered black hair was still drying and her face was clear and fresh and devoid of make-up...and she looked incredibly beautiful. 'You look—'

'Like Mackenzie?' Reggie shook her head and looked down at the demure clothes in disgust. 'No colour. No vibrance. No pizazz.' She snapped her fingers as she spoke, which only made Flynn laugh as he carried the shopping bags through to the kitchen. He dumped them on the table before turning to look at her once more.

'I mean, I love her and everything and I really do appreciate the loan of the clothes but we have absolutely nothing in common as far as how we dress,' she continued as she followed him.

'It's true that you prefer to wear bright colours,

sometimes even mixing and matching different print materials that ordinarily should *never* go together but somehow look completely perfect on you.'

Perfect? She brushed the thought aside. 'You're a textile expert, eh? Now, *that* I definitely didn't know. Please, continue, oh, wise fashionista.'

Flynn's eyes flashed with repressed humour and, while keeping a straight face, he slowly walked around her, murmuring and nodding as though deep in thought. 'Yes. Yes. I can see what you mean. It *is* rather conservative for the likes of Ms Regina Smith, General Surgeon Extraordinaire, but I think I can solve the dilemma quite easily.'

'You can?' She couldn't help the way she felt so incredibly self-conscious with him walking around her, looking her up and down, and although she knew they were only pretending, somehow his visual inspection had become more of an intimate caress. She fought against the sensation, determined not to spoil this lighthearted moment. They'd always been able to joke together, to tease each other in a good-natured way, and now that it was happening again she started to realise just how much she'd missed him.

'Oh, yes, indeedy I can.' He crossed to the bags he'd placed on the table and reached inside, pulling out a small white box. He held it out to her.

'What's this?' she asked.

'Open it.'

Dropping all pretence, Reggie accepted the gift box with surprise. It wasn't tied or secured in any way and after she gently eased the lid off she saw white tissue paper. She glanced at Flynn, who only nodded with encouragement. She moved the folded tissue paper aside to reveal a bright and beautiful Christmas-patterned silk scarf.

'Oh!' She stared at it in astonishment for a moment before carefully pulling it from the box. Flynn instantly took the box from her hands as she ran the silken threads through her fingers. 'Flynn. It's...' she met his gaze '...lovely.' To her astonishment, she felt tears begin to gather behind her eyes and she quickly looked away, desperate to pull herself together and gain some sort of control over her emotions. Always difficult when Flynn was so close.

'I thought you might need a bit of colour in your life, particularly this morning, and I couldn't go past the bright Christmas theme.'

'It's perfect. Thank you.' Reggie continued to sift the scarf through her fingers as she tried to ignore the lump in her throat. Then, out of nowhere, logical thought seemed to click in and she looked at him, angling her head to the side, a slight frown marring her brow. 'Wait a moment. It's not even eight o'clock in the morning. How did you manage to buy this when the shops aren't even open?'

Flynn shrugged. 'I know a guy.'

'Of course you do.' Reggie shook her head, remembering how easily things came to wealthy people. It annoyed her that the knowledge put a dampener on what was yet another thoughtful gesture from Flynn. He'd gone out of his way to do something nice for her and she shouldn't care about the logistics. Deciding to ignore it, she tied the scarf around her neck, the bright reds and greens instantly bringing more colour to her outfit.

'Definitely perfect.' Flynn stepped forward and fixed the back of her collar before bringing his fingers to his lips and blowing a kiss into the air. 'Very festive. The fashionista has done it again.' He raised one arm in the air with a flourish.

Reggie's previous annoyance instantly fled in light of his antics and she laughed. She'd always believed that if a person didn't want to be in a bad mood, they could simply decide not to be, that they had the power over their own emotions to change the way they were feeling, and that was exactly what she was going to do right now. She wasn't going to dwell on the fact that Flynn came from money, that he'd lived a pampered life, that his family's wealth had been one of the reasons for him breaking their engagement.

No. She was going to step forth into her new life. The life where she was Flynn's housemate for the next few weeks. The life where she had the opportunity to buy new things, to start afresh. The life where that fresh new start might even include Flynn.

CHAPTER FIVE

REGGIE TOLD HERSELF she didn't feel self-conscious driving to work with her new housemate, that she didn't care if people saw them pull into the doctors' car park together or that they walked side by side into the hospital and onto the ward for the early morning round. She and Flynn were friends and colleagues and it wasn't uncommon for friends and colleagues to carpool. So many people working here did it. Being with Flynn, constantly, was nothing to be remarked on.

'Whoa, Reggie,' Ingrid, the general surgical registrar, commented quietly as they waited in the nurses' station for the rest of the ward-round participants to arrive. 'Did I just see you arriving at work with Dr Gorgeous Legs?'

Reggie couldn't help but grin widely at the nickname. 'Dr Gorgeous Legs?' she asked with a hint of incredulity.

'Sure. Nice long legs that lead up to a firm torso and a perfectly handsome face.' Ingrid eyed Flynn as she spoke.

'You're almost licking your lips.'

'Who could blame me?' Ingrid sighed then looked pointedly at Reggie. 'So give. How did you score a lift with him?'

'My car's still being fixed at the garage, you know, after those joyriders smashed into it the other week.' She shook her head innocently, hoping to change the subject. 'There it was. Legally parked on the side of the road while I did my grocery shopping and, wham—the next minute it was destroyed as they smashed fair into it. Still, at least it can be repaired. After the fire and all last night, the last thing I would have wanted was to have to buy a new c—'

'Yes, yes. I'm sorry about your car and your apartment.' Ingrid impatiently waved her words away. 'That doesn't explain how Gorgeous Legs gave you a lift.'

'Oh. That's easy. Flynn and I are old friends.' Reggie said the words as matter-of-factly as possible, picking up a pen and pretending to study that day's ward-round sheet with great interest. Ingrid wasn't being sidetracked or fooled by Reggie's faked nonchalance.

Ingrid's eye brows almost hit her hairline. 'Really?' There was an insinuation in Ingrid's very interested tone and Reggie was sorely tempted to spin her a yarn, to say that they were actually a long-lost brother and sister, separated at birth. Or that Flynn had saved her life by donating a kidney. Flippant and funny. Anything to hide her true self behind a mask of bright happiness, but as she looked over to where Flynn was chatting with a heavily pregnant Geetha, who was doing her final ward round before handing over her patients to Flynn, Reggie realised that he deserved better.

'We worked together during our final year of general surgical training.'

'Oh.' Ingrid was clearly disappointed with her answer and as Geetha was calling the ward round to order, there was no time for the registrar to say anything else. Throughout the round Reggie frequently found herself standing beside Flynn, remembering past ward rounds they'd conducted together in that small Caribbean hospital.

'Do you remember the first time we did a ward round together?' he asked her as they walked towards the cafeteria to grab a quick coffee before their clinic started.

Reggie smiled. 'You were dressed in a three-piece suit.'

'You wore a bright yellow sundress.'

'We were working in the Caribbean, Flynn. It's hot there.'

'It was practically see-through, Reg. Gave my heart a mighty big flutter.'

She grinned at his words, hearing the teasing note. 'Really?'

'I'd been working in the UK, where it had been freezing cold and raining, before catching my flight. I literally got off the plane in the Caribbean, raced to the hospital and arrived three minutes before the ward round started. You were the first person I saw and you were…a vision of loveliness.'

'Oh.' She could feel her cheeks beginning to suffuse with colour at his sweet words.

'For a moment I thought I was hallucinating.'

'Really? You looked very uncomfortable.' She laughed nervously, trying to disguise the fact that his words had affected her. He'd really been that instantly attracted to her? She couldn't remember him telling her that. She gazed up at him, their eyes locking, silently communicating. The moment between them was starting to stretch, starting to change, starting to become more intense than she was ready for. She needed to lighten the mood somehow.

'I was.'

'But you were determined not to show it.'

'I was exceedingly stubborn back then.'

'Yes. Yes, you were.' As they stood in the cafeteria line, she smiled up at him. 'And very stiff and rigid.' She picked up his arm and gave it a shake. 'You're much more loosey-goosey now.'

'Loosey-goosey?' Flynn chuckled as he reached out with his free hand and straightened the bright Christmas scarf around her neck. He exhaled slowly as Reggie released his arm, their fingers brushing lightly, almost caressing. The smile started to disappear from his mouth as he continued to gently tug and pull the scarf, smoothing it with his fingers.

'All fixed, Mr Fashionista?'

It was the sound of her voice, a little softer, a little huskier than normal, that made him shift his gaze to encompass her. 'Yes,' he replied softly. 'Perfect. As usual.'

'Perfect?' There was that word again and Reggie cleared her throat, desperate to try and keep their previous light-hearted banter in her words.

'As usual,' he repeated, his intense gaze penetrating deeply into her soul.

'You thought I was perfect?' The words were barely a whisper and for a moment she wasn't even sure she'd spoken until he nodded, the movement small but definite.

'Always.'

'Oh.'

'Are you two moving forward in the line or do you mind if I cut in front of you?' the impatient male nurse said from behind them.

'Er...' Reggie blinked, looking away from Flynn, unable to believe she'd been standing in the busy hospital cafeteria line just staring at him. Her only saving grace was that he'd been staring back at her. Flynn stepped aside and gestured for the nurse to precede them.

'We're not in as much of a rush as you. Please,' he offered politely. The nurse rolled his eyes before walking between them and advancing before them in the line.

'You really are more...I don't know.' Reggie shrugged her shoulders and gave him a quirky smile. 'Relaxed, I guess, is the best word to describe you.'

'Plus, I'm not wearing a three-piece suit.'

'True,' she said, indicating his navy trousers, white shirt and tie, which had a parachuting Santa Claus on it. 'Very loosey-goosey.'

'And...' he remarked, picking up the end of his tie and pressing it.

A moment later Reggie heard 'Jingle Bells' playing in an electronic, tinny way. It lasted for a whole ten seconds and she couldn't help but giggle.

'Your tie plays "Jingle Bells"?' She was amused but also pleasantly surprised. When they'd first met all those years ago he would never have worn anything like this.

'Yes.'

'Your tie plays "Jingle Bells" and you're only showing me this *now*.'

Flynn grinned widely as they edged forward in the line. 'I knew if I'd shown you before ward round you would have wanted to play it for every patient and ward round would have taken way too long.'

'That's exactly what I would have wanted to do.' She pushed a hand through her hair and shook her head in stunned amazement.

'I know you, Reggie.'

'So you keep reminding me.'

As she said the words she felt the smile begin to

slip because there was still so much he *didn't* know. How would Flynn react when he found out about her past, about what had happened to her, what she'd lived through? She'd managed to hide it from him before but would it make any difference now to their burgeoning relationship?

After the way they'd just openly stared at each other, it was clear the attraction was alive and well and yet she had no real idea what she felt for him, apart from enjoying his company, and right at this moment she wasn't sure she was ready for that to end. Flynn made her feel special and pretty and feminine and no other man had ever been able to achieve all three…and most certainly not with a simple lift of an eyebrow.

They ordered their coffees, Flynn paying for them before she could pull her money from her pocket, and after thanking him, something she seemed to be doing a lot of lately, they headed to Outpatients.

'Now you're both late?' Clara said as they walked in together. She pointed to the different piles of case notes waiting for them both. They grinned at the outpatient clerk. 'One day I'd love it if clinic could actually start on time,' Clara said pointedly.

'We'll try and make it a Christmas miracle,' Reggie promised as she scooped up the notes, ensuring she didn't spill her coffee in the process.

'I'll believe it when I see it,' Clara joked, smiling and shaking her head in bemusement.

Today Reggie was in no hurry to avoid Flynn. Instead, she was delighted every time they met in the corridor or headed out to call in a patient at the same time. It was as they were almost finished with clinic that she received a call from Bergan in Accident and Emergency.

'Reggie? I need you.'

'OK. Can you give me fifteen minutes or—?'

'Now,' Bergan interrupted, and before she rang off she added as an afterthought, 'And bring Flynn. I need him, too.'

'OK.' Reggie hung up and headed out into the corridor. Instead of calling in her last patient, she knocked on Flynn's consulting-room door. They'd have to leave it to Ingrid to finish up with the clinic list but, thankfully, there were only two or three patients left to go.

'Yes?' he called, and when she entered it was to find him and one of the clinic nurses helping their elderly female patient to her feet, the nurse ensuring the woman's walking frame was stable. 'Ah, Dr Smith. Good timing. Could you hold the door for Mrs Baladucci, please?'

'Certainly.' Reggie held the door as the nurse and Mrs Baladucci exited the consulting room, then she turned to face Flynn, who was quickly writing up the case notes before closing them and adding them to the 'completed' pile.

'Let me guess. Emergency?' Flynn asked.

'How did you know?' She stared at him for a moment before shaking her head in astonishment.

'You have a…certain look in your eyes and around the corners of your mouth whenever there's an unknown medical problem.'

'I do?' Reggie touched her fingers to the corners of her mouth, feeling a little self-conscious.

'I know you.'

'Oh, will you stop saying that? Please?' She spread her arms wide. 'There's actually quite a lot you don't know about me, Flynn. Yes, you knew me six years ago and, yes, we were very close and, no, I may not have changed in essentials, but will you stop constantly pointing out that you know me because, in reality, you don't.' The words tumbled out of her mouth before she could stop them.

Flynn stared at her in surprise. 'I didn't realise it upset you so much.'

'Well, it does.' Reggie gritted her teeth for a moment. 'I don't know what you want from me, Flynn. I don't know if the offer to help relocate my neighbours or having me stay at your place comes with any sort of strings attached but I just can't deal with too much more right now.'

'There are no strings attached,' he said quickly. 'And what I want from you, Reg, is quite simple.' He stood and looked her directly in the eyes. 'I want your forgiveness.'

'Forgi—' She stopped, too stunned to speak. She couldn't remember anyone ever asking her for her forgiveness before, especially someone who had hurt her so badly.

'So…we're needed in A and E?' he asked, breaking the moment and tidying the desk.

'Y-yes.' Reggie blinked, working hard to compartmentalise her thoughts. Flynn wanted her forgiveness. Bergan needed her in A and E. Patients. Trauma. Expertise. That's what she needed to focus on right now and, dragging in a breath, she pushed her personal thoughts aside. 'Retrieval team.'

'I'm part of the retrieval team? I don't remember—'

'Bergan said she needed you.' Reggie threw her arms in the air in complete exasperation. 'That's all I know.' Then she turned and headed out, wanting to get down to A and E as soon as possible so she could concentrate on something other than the way Flynn was constantly spinning her first one way then the other. She wished he'd stop because the motion was starting to make her feel ill.

In A and E, several of the retrieval team had already changed into the blue and yellow jumpsuits that stated they were part of the medical team at Sunshine General. Reggie headed over to where Bergan was gathering everyone together in the nurses' station, feeling rather than knowing that Flynn was directly behind her.

She tried hard to switch off her awareness of him and focus on whatever Bergan had called them down to assist with. Professional. She needed to be professional. After all, she'd worked alongside Flynn before; in fact, they'd worked exceptionally well together in the Caribbean…and that had been part of the problem. Too good, too close, too quickly.

Bergan cleared her throat and everyone around fell silent, waiting for her to speak. 'The key players are here. We're just waiting for Mackenzie but she's just getting out of Theatre so we'll begin without her.' Bergan pointed to the computer monitor, which was revealing a picture of the main beach in Maroochydore. 'We've had a report from the surf lifeguards that a shark has been sighted on the beach. They've closed the area but have just spotted a person, out to sea, floating. One male, approximately in late fifties to sixties. They're sending out a boat now and request immediate assistance.'

She turned to Flynn and Reggie. 'You two, go in the chopper. You both have the relevant experience when it comes to shark attacks, having treated and operated on victims before. I want you at the scene, stat. The instant they have that body out of the water, you need to be standing by.'

'Is there just the one victim?' Reggie asked, her mind

going through the different injury scenarios they might be facing.

'That's the report at this time. Go and change. Get to that chopper.' With that, Bergan turned her gaze to the rest of the team. 'Everyone else, listen for your posts.'

'Change rooms are this way,' Reggie said, before Flynn could ask. They walked quickly along the corridor, down the side of A and E towards the changing rooms. 'Retrieval suits will be just inside the door. Once you're changed, we'll meet back in the corridor, grab the retrieval gear and head up to the chopper.'

'I guess all that experience in the Caribbean has come in handy. I hope I can remember what we need to do,' Flynn remarked as they hurried along. 'I've been working very much inland for the past few years.'

Reggie smiled at him reassuringly as they reached the changing room doors. 'You'll be fine and if you forget, just ask me.'

'I'll do that,' he promised, as he punched in the code for the male changing rooms at the same time she tapped in the code for the female changing rooms. 'See you in five minutes.'

'Or less,' she remarked, pushing open the door.

Ten minutes later, they were both changed, seated in the chopper with their medical retrieval backpacks and ready for take-off.

'Any word from the surf lifeguards?' Reggie asked their pilot through the headset.

'I'll patch you through to Bergan,' he replied.

'What's the latest?' Reggie asked a moment later as they headed out towards the sea.

'They've got the man in the boat. Left arm is partially detached, incision bites to left side of abdomen,' came Bergan's clear words. 'There is also a report of a second victim. Young girl, twelve years of age. Lacerations to right side, unconscious, right foot missing.'

Reggie closed her eyes as Bergan spoke, knowing full well that Flynn could hear every word through his own headset. She tried to picture the victims' wounds, tried to keep her mind focused, imagining herself moving through the motions of treatment. At times like these they couldn't afford to think about the personal, about those poor people who had suffered such horror. In order to remain professional, they needed to remain detached.

'The boat should be on the beach in two minutes.'

'What's our ETA?' Flynn asked the pilot, watching Reggie closely, whose eyes were tightly shut. He knew she was trying to think things through, to imagine the wounds and the treatment they'd require. He could also remember the first time she'd been like this. Their very first retrieval together.

They'd been sitting in an ambulance, being driven from the hospital on Sint Maarten, towards a luxury hotel where several guests had been crippled with a gastro bug. As they'd been the only surgical residents at the hospital, it had fallen to them to treat the patients. Flynn had met Reggie only the day before and while he'd been instantly attracted to her, he hadn't been at all sure how she performed under pressure.

'She's far too happy for her own good and although she did well in ward round, I have to wonder if she's got what it takes to cope in emergency situations,' he'd told Violet when he'd spoken to her on the phone after his first day.

'I'm sure she'll be fine, Flynn,' Violet had responded. The two had known each other since they'd been toddlers, their mothers the best of friends, and Violet had been the closest thing he'd had to a sister. Their mothers had always said that one day the two of them were destined to marry, but both he and Violet had laughed it off, preferring to remain just good friends. 'If she's a qualified doctor and doing the same surgical training you are, then she must have some smarts,' Violet had wisely pointed out.

Flynn had frowned, unable to believe the instant attraction he'd felt towards his new colleague. Perhaps doubting her abilities was his way of dealing with that unwanted attraction? At any rate, he'd hoped she was good because he hadn't really fancied having to carry the weight of running the surgical team on Sint Maarten on his own for the next six weeks. 'I'm still not convinced.'

'Anyway,' Violet had continued, 'Tell me about the more relaxed pace of life. Nice and slow? Sunshine all the time? I hope so because seriously I thought your parents were going to pressure you into a coronary if you hadn't left.'

'You're exaggerating, Violet,' he'd returned.

'Six weeks of sun, surf and drinks with little umbrellas in them. Utter bliss.'

'Sunburn, sand stuck everywhere and incompetent colleagues.'

Violet laughed at him, not taking his words seriously. 'She must be pretty if you're already labelling her as incompetent. You always do that, Flynn. It's a protective measure. Any time you feel out of your depth, you look for the negative.'

'I do?'

'Look, Flynn, just promise me you'll stop burning the candle at both ends and try to enjoy yourself. Get to know this colleague of yours. What did you say her name was?'

'Regina Smith. Although she's already informed me that she hates being called Regina, that she much prefers Reggie—like she's some sort of trucker. Then she throws her arms around me in one of those uncomfortable friendship-hug things, telling me what a wonderful time we'll have working together. Far too happy for her own good.'

Violet wasn't able to stop laughter from flowing down the telephone line. 'She sounds fantastic, Flynn, and perhaps just what you need for the next few weeks. A little holiday romance, eh?'

'Bite your tongue. You know I'm not interested in any sort of relationship. Not with the pressure our parents are putting on us.'

'It'll never happen, Flynn. You and I are destined to be best friends. Nothing more. Now go. I have a feeling that this Reggie Smith may just surprise you.'

And she did. As they travelled in the ambulance, heading towards that luxury hotel, Reggie's eyes were closed as though she was trying to catch up on her sleep.

'Conserving your energy?' he asked.

'No.' She spoke the single word before opening one eye to look at him, the corners of her lips turning upwards. 'Concentrating.' She closed her eye and lapsed back into silence.

'Er...OK. Well, would you like to talk about what sort of scenarios we might encounter and how you envisage us handling the situation to ensure an effective and prompt outcome?'

'That's what I'm doing,' she replied. 'I like to close my eyes and picture the situation, visualise myself treating the patient. That way I know exactly what equipment I need and the best way to handle things.'

'You...*picture* yourself doing this?'

'Yes. Try it.' She opened one eye again and looked directly at him. 'Close your eyes.'

'I don't think—'

'We have another five minutes before arrival. Just try it at least.' She closed her eyes again and, feeling utterly stupid and knowing he probably looked ridiculous, Flynn eventually closed his eyes.

'Let's say the patient complains of right-sided abdominal pain with localised tenderness in the middle. I see myself palpating their abdomen, ensuring it isn't appendicitis or hernia. Although there's an outbreak of a gastro bug, it doesn't mean that one of our patients isn't suffering from that but is rather suffering from something far more serious. Not that I'm trying to imply that gastroenteritis isn't a serious condition but simply pointing out that we need to be on top of things.' She paused to take a breath but before she could start again he jumped in.

'You're a talker,' he stated, opening his eyes, feeling mildly silly for agreeing to do things her way but impressed she'd actually managed to get him to comply.

Reggie's grin was bright and wide, like her gorgeous blue eyes as she opened them to look at him. She leaned forward in her seat, as far as the seat belt would allow and looked directly into his eyes. 'I've been told the only way to shut me up is to kiss me.' She waggled her eyebrows up and down suggestively and then sat back in her seat and openly laughed at the stunned look on his face. 'Relax, Flynn. I don't bite.' She winked at him. 'Not unless you want me to.'

The old cliché somehow sounded fresh coming from

Reggie's lips and it was only then he realised he'd been staring at her mouth, as though his thoughts were more than willing to follow her lead.

And indeed, the first time he had kissed her had been to shut her up. He couldn't remember what she'd been talking about but he did remember not hearing a word of what she'd been saying, more fascinated by the way her lips moved, wanting desperately to kiss them, to show her just how desirable she was.

Now, many years later, with so much water having flowed rapidly under the bridge between them, Flynn wanted nothing more than to lean forward and kiss those incredibly perfect lips of hers...lips that fitted so snugly against his own. How he'd yearned for them over the years. How he wanted to pick up where they'd left off. How he wished he'd been stronger back then and had stood up for what he'd really wanted out of life.

'Preparing for descent,' the chopper pilot said.

'Copy that,' Reggie returned, and opened her eyes. She looked directly at Flynn. 'Ready?'

'Yeah.' He nodded his head for emphasis and cleared his throat, unsure whether she'd heard him properly through her headphones. He needed to pull it together. To be professional. He knew Reggie—and their patients—were counting on him but sometimes it was difficult to be around her, especially when there were so many memories of their time together intruding into his thoughts.

As the chopper landed and they disembarked, Flynn tried not to notice the way even the blue and yellow overalls made Reggie look sexy. Carrying their gear, they headed over to where the surf lifeguards' boat was being pulled up onto the sand. Reggie was taking the lead on this one and he'd learned, that first day, as they'd treated over thirty patients at the hotel for various complaints, that she was indeed an exceptional doctor.

Bright, talented and absolutely gorgeous. A lethal combination and one he was far from being immune to.

CHAPTER SIX

ON THE BEACH, the surf lifeguards had set up a shield to give them some privacy while the man, whose name was only given as Kev, was carried from the lifeboat to where Flynn and Reggie were opening their emergency backpacks, ready to get to work.

'Establish IV line, get that plasma up and going, stat,' she stated, and Flynn nodded.

'Agreed.' Although they both knew what they were doing, it was important to communicate effectively and clearly exactly what procedures they were undertaking.

As soon as Kev was placed in front of them, they both had their gloves on. As Kev was wearing a wetsuit, Flynn took out the heavy-duty scissors and immediately began cutting away the neoprene fabric so they could better see what they were dealing with. After peeling away the section from his chest, most of which was covered in blood, Reggie hooked her stethoscope into her ears to check Kev's heart rate while Flynn grabbed a large bandage and applied pressure to Kev's left arm, ensuring it was as secure as possible to assist with stemming the bleeding.

'Hi, Kev,' she said to the man, who was semi-conscious. 'I'm Dr Reggie Smith with Sunshine General. This is Dr Flynn Jamieson. We're here to help you.'

She smiled at him as she unhooked the stethoscope. With the paramedics on the scene, one of them came over and was able to hold Kev's head stable until they could get a neck brace onto him.

'The girl.' Kev spoke the words through gritted teeth as Flynn picked up a penlight torch from his medical kit and performed Kev's neurological observations. As they worked, both Flynn and Reggie called their findings to each other.

'Heart rate is elevated.'

'Pupils equal and reacting to light. Best to put the line in his foot,' Flynn remarked, before looking down at Kev. 'The girl's been found. The surf lifeguards are bringing her in now.'

'She was…being taken farther…out to sea. Had…to save her.' His words were disjointed but understandable, which showed his cognitive function was clearly working.

'You did great, Kev. Now I need you to try and relax. We're here to help you.' Reggie was taking the tubing she required from the sterile packaging. She checked both feet for pulses and reported they were both there. She also asked Kev to wiggle all his toes for her and although it hurt, he was able to do as she asked. 'You'll feel just a little scratch,' she told him as she prepared to insert the cannula into his foot.

'I've felt more…than that today,' he retorted. 'What… what are you doing?'

'You've lost a lot of blood, Kev,' Flynn told him. 'We need to replace those fluids as soon as possible. Once we have some fluids into you, we can give you something for the pain. Can you wiggle the fingers on your right hand for me?'

'I'm not important,' Kev told them.

'I beg to differ,' Reggie replied, as one of the other paramedics came over to help. She left him to finish off inserting the drip and turned her attention to Kev's abdomen. 'I just need to have a little look around, see what the damage is, and then we can give you something for the pain,' she told him.

'The girl. The girl...is all that's important,' he said, his teeth gritted in pain. 'Need to save the girl.'

'You did save her,' Flynn reassured him.

'I did?' At this news, Kev seemed to relax a bit. He closed his eyes. 'Couldn't save my own girl but...this is good.'

Reggie and Flynn briefly looked at each other, wondering what on earth Kev could be talking about. The bite marks on Kev's abdomen were clear but deep. Flynn had already packed one of the puncture wounds with gauze and Reggie grabbed another bandage from her kit and applied pressure to one area on Kev's lower left abdomen.

'Hold this,' she instructed the paramedic, who had now finished setting up the drip. 'I think it's time we gave you something for the pain,' she told Kev. 'Are you allergic to anything?'

'No. No, but had a heart attack...six years ago now... but good since,' Kev replied, unable to shake his head as the paramedic was now attaching a neck brace to keep Kev's head as still as possible.

'And you're not taking anything? No fish oil?'

'Vegan now,' he told her. 'Flaxseed oil.'

'Good. That's all fine.' Reggie reached into her medical kit for the syringe that had already been drawn up with the medication and clearly labelled. 'Check ten milligrams of morphine,' she said.

Flynn glanced over, checked and confirmed the

medication she was about to give Kev, before replying, 'Check.'

'There you go, Kev,' she told him as she administered the medication via the butterfly cannula. A few moments later Kev's features began to relax.

Now that Kev was out of pain, Flynn was able to increase his investigation of the abdomen. 'Not sure if the patient has voided, given the wetsuit, but possible bladder and kidney rupture, large and small intestinal damage but both lungs appear fine. Suspected fracture to left neck of femur and probable pelvic bone damage.'

'And the arm?' Reggie asked, after she'd rechecked Kev's heart rate. She took the stethoscope out of her ears and met Flynn's gaze. He didn't need to say anything—the look in his eyes told her that the arm didn't look at all good and the chances of Kev keeping it were minimal.

'Took the brunt of the attack.' Kev's words were barely audible. She nodded, indicating she understood exactly what he was not saying. The salty sea wind was whipping around them and she was glad of the screens the paramedics had erected. The lifeguards on the beach were keeping the onlookers at bay as best they could. When a shark alarm was raised, it tended to send a thread of panic through everyone who was around, whether they'd been in the water nor not.

'The boat? The boat?' Kev asked, still concerned, even though the morphine was definitely working. 'Is it in? Where's the girl?'

'The sea's a bit choppy,' one of the paramedics reported. 'They've got her in the boat. They're on their way,' he reassured their patient. Still, Kev seemed slightly agitated again. Something was clearly bothering him.

'Wasn't supposed to...turn out like this,' he mumbled, and Flynn frowned.

'Let's get him back to the hospital so he can be prepared for surgery. With the sounds of sirens in the distance, it appears the cavalry is on the way so we can leave the girl to Bergan and her team.'

'Good thinking.' Reggie pulled her walkie-talkie from the medical kit and contacted the helicopter pilot. 'You ready to head back?'

'Got a patient for me?' he asked.

'Copy that. Name is Kev—that's all I have at the moment. We'll stretcher him now. ETA six minutes.'

Now that the transfer was organised, Reggie did a final check of Kev's vitals, pleased to see he was responding well to the fluids and pain medication, and yet he still seemed uneasy. Then again, he'd just been bitten by a shark but her intuition told her it was more than that.

'Good news, Kev,' she said brightly. 'We're getting you off the beach.' She checked the bandages they'd applied, pleased with his situation. They'd managed to get to Kev as quickly as possible and even though he was in his late fifties, it was clear that he was the type of man who looked after his health.

'Wait. Wait.' Kev's eyes snapped open, the look in them as wild as the sea. 'The girl. Is she OK? I need to know. Please? Please?'

'They're still coming in, Kev, but the other staff from Sunshine General have arrived. They're brilliant and know what they're doing. They'll take good care of her.'

'We need to get you back, Kev. Your abdominal injuries need further treatment and surgical interven—' Flynn started.

'I need to give you…a message,' Kev interrupted, his tone forceful.

'For whom?' Reggie asked, trying to use her calming voice to placate him a little. They needed him transferred as soon as possible but she didn't want to risk agitating him further by not giving him the respect he deserved.

'Write it down.'

'It's all right. We can do this back at the hospital. You're nice and stable now and we'd like to keep it that way,' she told him.

'Please? I need to give you a message…for my wife.'

'You're going to be fine, Kev. You can tell her yourself when you see her.'

'No. No. She hates me.' He closed his eyes at the words. 'Write it down.'

Reggie looked across at Flynn, who shrugged one shoulder. 'He's the patient. It's his call.' She nodded and pulled off her bloodied gloves before reaching into the medical kit, finding a pen but no paper.

'Wait a moment,' one of the paramedics said, unzipping his overalls and digging into his trouser pocket before pulling out a clean napkin. 'Use this.'

'Thanks.' Reggie accepted it from him then looked at Kev. 'What do you want me write?'

'I hope saving this girl…makes up for not saving ours.' Kev closed his eyes as he spoke and for a moment Reggie's throat closed over, an immediate lump forming there, which was difficult to swallow over. Kev had lost his daughter? 'Did you get that?'

'Uh…' She quickly scribbled down his words. 'Yes.'

'Also, tell her to remember…remember Coffs Harbour at New Year's…and the dingo dance.'

'Dingo dance?' Reggie raised her eyebrows as she looked at Kev. 'Sounds interesting.'

'You got that?' he asked again, and she nodded.

'All written down,' Reggie reassured him, before tucking the pen and paper into a pocket in her retrieval suit. 'What's your wife's name?' she asked.

'Michaela.'

'OK. That's all done. Now, I really think it's time we get you onto that chopper and back to the hospital.' Reggie smiled down at him.

Once again Kev seemed to relax a bit more but he looked determinedly at her and asked, 'You'll let me know about the girl?'

'As soon as we know anything, we'll let you know,' she told him. With the assistance of the paramedics they transferred Kev to a stretcher. 'Take him over to the chopper. I'll just quickly debrief Bergan and Mackenzie,' she told Flynn, who nodded. She watched for a moment as the screens were lowered and the lifeguards did their best to stop onlookers from taking photographs on their cellphones. The police were there as well, a few of them clearing the way for Kev to be carried to the helicopter.

As she started to walk away, a police officer came running up to her.

'Is it all right to talk to the patient now? We need to try and piece together what happened.'

'He's been given morphine and Penthrane so he might be a little vague on details but give it a go,' she encouraged. 'We need to have wheels up in five minutes.'

'Understood,' the police officer said, and headed off after Flynn and the paramedics who were carrying Kev's stretcher towards the chopper.

Reggie quickly trudged her way through the sand towards Bergan, the wind still whipping at her hair. It was at times like these she was glad she'd cut her hair short. Reggie looked around at all the beachgoers, some packing their things up and leaving, others standing behind the area the police had cordoned off, teenagers taking photographs with their cameras and cellphones.

Emergency personnel were doing their jobs, working together like a well-oiled machine. Reggie hadn't even been aware of the police arriving but without them who knew how many people would have tried to sneak a look around those screens while she and Flynn had been treating Kev.

'We are a curious species,' she murmured to herself as Bergan walked over to her, the two meeting out of earshot of onlookers. 'Hey, there.'

'Your patient all ready for transfer?' Bergan asked.

'Yes. Left arm almost completely torn off. Amputation is a definite consideration but I'll get John to consult when we get back to the hospital.' Reggie pointed to where the surf lifesaving boat, after battling high waves brought on by an oncoming storm, was finally reaching the beach. 'You and Mackenzie OK to take care of the girl?'

'Yes. You'll probably be in Theatres by the time we return but I'll keep you informed.'

'Kev—my patient—was really concerned about the girl so I'd appreciate that.'

'No problem.'

Reggie turned and jogged towards the chopper, looking back to see them lifting the young girl from the boat and carrying her to a second screened-off area, away from prying eyes. She certainly hoped the girl was strong enough to make it through.

'Excuse me!' a woman called from behind the police tape, and when Reggie looked at her, the woman quickly ducked beneath the tape and ran towards her. 'I'm looking for Kev.'

'I'm sorry,' Reggie said, her tone filled with apology. 'You'll need to wait behind the tape.'

'I'm his…er…wife. Michaela.'

Reggie nodded. 'Yes. He's told me about you. Come with me. You can ride in the chopper with us.'

Michaela face turned pale. 'So he really has been attacked. I thought it was a bad joke.'

'We need to go now,' Reggie urged, breaking into a jog and urging Michaela along. 'Kev needs immediate surgery.'

Michaela shook her head. 'I never come to the beach. I can't stand it but he loves it.'

'Never mind about that now.'

'But you don't understand. I only came down so he could sign the divorce papers. I've been pressuring him to do it for months but he kept refusing.'

They'd reached the chopper and Reggie's heart went out to the woman as she read guilt and remorse in Michaela's eyes. She placed her hand on Michaela's shoulder, her words warm. 'Focus on being brave for Kev. It doesn't matter what's happened in the past, he needs you now. Can you do that?'

Michaela seemed to consider that for a moment before she nodded. 'Yes.'

'Good. Let's get you into the chopper.'

'Why does everything bad happen at Christmas?' Michaela muttered as she climbed into the chopper, sitting down and allowing herself to be strapped in by the pilot. Reggie introduced her to Flynn, who had just finished doing Kev's observations.

'Can he hear me?' Michaela asked, as the rotors of the helicopter started to whirr above them.

'He's been given pain relief to make transport easier,' Reggie said apologetically as she strapped herself in and donned her headphones.

'Six minutes and we'll be at the hospital,' the pilot announced, then the chopper lifted smoothly upwards.

'Call through to the hospital and have John Watson standing by,' Reggie instructed.

'Copy that,' the pilot returned.

'Is that Mackenzie's husband?' Flynn asked, and Reggie nodded.

'Excellent orthopaedic surgeon,' she told him as both she and Flynn kept a close eye on Kev's condition. Thankfully, the trip was non-eventful and John was there waiting for them when the pilot landed the helicopter safely on the roof above the A and E department. A short lift ride down and they were wheeling Kev's bed through to the treatment room. After transferring him to a hospital bed, Reggie and Flynn performed observations again, Michaela standing in the corner out of the way, watching and listening in disbelief as Reggie spoke clearly, giving details of Kev's condition to the A and E staff, as well as John.

'I can't believe it. I just can't believe it,' Michaela kept repeating. Kev was still drowsy from the analgesics and it was clear he needed to go to Theatre as soon as possible. Reggie took Michaela out of the treatment room, down the corridor to a small waiting room, where she started to explain the operation to her.

'Michaela, we need you to sign the consent forms as you are his next of kin.'

'But we're supposed to be getting divorced. I have the papers here for him to sign and then that's it.'

'However…' Reggie tried to remain calm, to get her point across in the most straightforward way because the longer they had to delay taking Kev to Theatre, the worse the outcome would be for him. 'In the eyes of the law you are still listed as his next of kin.' Reggie looked into Michaela's eyes. 'I know all of this has come as a shock but he really does need surgery and we can't progress until—'

'Dr Reggie Smith. Dr Reggie Smith,' came the call over the A and E intercom. 'Code Blue, TR One.'

'What?' Reggie was on her feet and racing back towards trauma room one, her mind going faster than her body as she thought through a thousand different scenarios in the thirty seconds it took her to return. 'What happened?' she asked as she pulled on a pair of gloves and a protective disposable gown.

One of the A and E nurses was performing cardiac massage on Kev.

'Blood pressure dropped. We lost output. He went into defib,' Flynn announced, as he prepared to push fluids, John readying the crash cart. 'Vitals dropped suddenly.'

Reggie was checking Kev's pupils. 'Come on, Kev. Stay with me. You can do it.' She shook her head. 'Not reacting to light.'

'Give me one of adrenaline,' Flynn ordered, as the nurse continued cardiac massage, another of the nurses bagging Kev to pump air into his lungs.

Reggie checked for a pulse and when she couldn't find one Flynn put his stethoscope into his ears and listened for a heartbeat.

'Nothing.' Flynn shook his head and glanced at Reggie. She nodded encouragingly, her eyes eager. 'Push fluids. Get ready to shock him.' Flynn looked at John, who nodded.

'Come on, Kev. Come on. You've come too far. You're a hero, Kev. An absolute hero,' she told him, as she watched Flynn administer the fluids. She closed her eyes for a second, wishing for a miracle, but even she knew the situation was bad. Kev had lost too much blood and even though they were continuing to do everything they possibly could to revive him, there was no guarantee he'd make it through surgery.

'Charging,' John said.

'Clear!' Flynn called, and everyone stepped back from the patient. 'No output.'

'Shock him again,' Reggie instructed, and again John charged the machine.

'Clear!' Flynn called once more, and after the shock had been administered, Reggie pressed her fingers to Kev's carotid pulse.

'Again,' she instructed.

'Reggie—' Flynn began.

'Again!' There was desperation in her words.

'Charging,' John called.

'Clear!' Flynn said, but after the third time there was still no output. 'I'm calling it.'

Flynn met Reggie's gaze, holding it for what seemed an eternity. She knew it was the right thing to do, that Kev had already been through so much, that he simply hadn't been able to fight any longer. He'd done his bit. He'd saved a twelve-year-old girl's life and he was a hero.

Flynn walked round to where she stood and put both hands on her shoulders, looking intently into her eyes. 'I'm sorry, Reg.'

'We did our job.'

'Do you want me to talk to his wife?'

'No.' She patted the pockets of her retrieval suit, looking for the napkin on which she'd written Kev's last words. 'I'll do it.'

'I'll go with you. Support is always good at a time like this.'

Reggie nodded and walked on wooden legs down towards the small room where she'd left Michaela not that long ago. Flynn's nearness really was comforting and she momentarily wondered whether he hadn't been offering support for *her* rather than for Kev's wife.

With the bright and cheerful Christmas music playing softly through the hospital's system, they entered the waiting room and just the forlorn look on Reggie's face must have adequately conveyed the situation to Michaela as the other woman instantly burst into tears.

'We did everything we could,' Reggie said, the words sounding hollow and inadequate as Michaela crumpled into a chair. Reggie put her hand on the other woman's shoulder, wanting to offer her support. 'His heart couldn't handle the stress of the attack. He passed away a few minutes ago.'

'No. No. This isn't the way it was supposed to happen.'

Reggie swallowed and looked up at Flynn, who nodded encouragingly for her to continue. She held the napkin between her fingers and looked down at the words she'd scribbled there not that long ago. 'He did leave a message he wanted me to pass on to you.' Reggie paused for a moment, not sure she could get the words past her lips but knowing she had to. 'He said he hoped saving the little girl today made up for not saving yours.'

At that, Michaela let loose with a fresh round of tears and Flynn quickly offered her some more tissues. It was incredibly difficult in these circumstances to know what to do or say and although they'd been trained in how to handle these sorts of situations, having the theoretical knowledge and watching someone's heart break into pieces because a loved one had passed away were two very different things.

'He said for you to remember Coffs Harbour at New Year's and the dingo dance.'

Michaela raised her head, hiccupping as she spoke. 'Why on earth would he say that?' she asked, blowing her nose amidst the tears.

Reggie shrugged, unsure what the relevance was. She was about to say she didn't know when Flynn spoke.

'Perhaps he wanted your last memory of him to be a happy one,' Flynn said, his voice deep and soft and filled with compassion.

Surprise lit Michaela's eyes. 'Oh.' Then she nodded. 'The dingo dance.' A small smile touched her quivering lips. 'He was so funny that night.'

'Is there someone we can call to come and be with you?'

Michaela took her phone from her handbag and nodded. 'I can do it.'

'OK. I'll get one of the nurses to come and bring you a drink. We'll be back as soon as possible.'

'Yes. Of course. You must be busy.' Michaela nodded and dabbed at her eyes with a fresh tissue. 'I don't know how you do it, how you cope.'

The lump was back in Reggie's throat and after they exited the room she quickly walked down one of the side corridors of A and E, needing to have a moment or two to herself. Bergan's office was down this secluded corridor and she quickly dug around in her pocket for her hospital pass card, but her fingers seemed to have turned into sausages. She needed the escape, to slip into Bergan's room, to cry and let the pain out, but the tears were already beginning to flow.

'Just let them go,' Flynn's voice said from behind her, and she jumped a little, not having heard him follow her. She turned and in the next instant she was in his arms, their firm warmth providing her with a protective shelter from the stormy emotions pounding at her heart.

'I've got you, Reg. I've got you,' he murmured softly near her ear, but as he spoke, Reggie could hear the thickness in his tone and as she buried her face into his chest, her body racked with sobs, she realised that Flynn was also shedding a few tears.

She was touched at this deeply personal, deeply sensitive side to him that she couldn't remember seeing before. They'd worked together on patients before, they'd lost patients before, but in all the time she'd spent with him he'd always managed to keep a close rein on his most intimate emotions.

Now he was sharing them with her and she couldn't help but feel…quite privileged.

CHAPTER SEVEN

REGGIE WASN'T SURE how long they stood there, their arms wrapped around each other, supporting each other. The job they did wasn't easy. It was bad enough when they were in Theatre and things didn't go their way, the patient dying during surgery, but to have gone out to the beach, to have spent time with Kev, having him confide in her, giving her the message to pass onto Michaela... and then to lose him.

Yes, it hurt, but it also felt incredibly good to have Flynn's strong arms about her. The pain was there but the fact that it was shared really did provide a level of comfort. It had been so long since anyone had just held her, without a hidden agenda, without wanting anything from her. Flynn was offering her comfort and she hoped in some way she was giving him back just the same.

She had no idea how long they stood there and a part of her never wanted it to end but she knew it must. It was their job to pull themselves together, to head back into the fray, as it were, and to help someone else who was still alive and who needed their expertise.

Slowly Reggie's tears started to subside but she was more than happy to stay where she was, at least for the moment. The memory of having Flynn's arms around her...of the way he would sometimes rub his thumbs in small circles in her lower back, giving her a gentle and sensual massage. Would he do that now? Did he want to do that?

Before the emergency, he'd asked for her forgiveness. The fact that he'd done that and also the way he'd been so incredibly thoughtful and helpful and wonderful and supportive was making it far too easy for her to fall in love with him all over again.

She knew he was here at Sunshine General covering Geetha's maternity leave but then what? What were his plans once Geetha returned in six months' time? There were just too many questions. Too many emotions. Too much…Flynn. She knew she needed to pull back, to try and find some sort of perspective where he was concerned, although how she was going to do that she had no clue.

Feeling a little better, Reggie started shifting slowly in his arms. She was becoming far too aware of how perfect his torso was, how he smelled of that deep, earthy spice that had always been intoxicating to her senses, and how she wanted nothing more than to ease back, lift her head and have him press his lips to hers.

He'd done it time and time again in the past and as his arms loosened, allowing her to shift a little more, she couldn't help but look up at him. His gaze automatically dipped to take in the contours of her mouth, the atmosphere between them changing from one of supportive colleagues to one of experienced familiarity.

She looked into his gorgeous eyes, hooded by those gorgeous long lashes, his straight nose, his cleft chin and his slightly parted lips. His arms were no longer protective and supportive but instead were bands of warmth, heating her up all over. Didn't the man have any idea just how powerful his hold was over her? She wanted him to kiss her, to follow through on the urge that seemed to be so tangible between them you could have cut it with a knife.

'Reg.' Even the way he spoke her name was filled with repressed desire. 'I really want to kiss you.'

At his words she gasped, her lips parting and her eyes widening at the bold but honest statement. Her hands were still halfway around his back from holding him close while she'd wept but now she brought them around to the front, to rest against his chest as she continued to look at him.

She really wasn't sure what to say or do because although she was longing to have his mouth pressed to hers once again, knowing she would be able to experience those thrilling sensations only Flynn had ever been able to evoke, she also remembered the pain he'd put her through when he'd broken her heart. She could forgive him. She knew that but could she trust him with her heart again? Was his desire to kiss her simply born from the moment they were sharing or was it something deeper?

He lifted his hand to run his fingers through her short dark hair. 'I like this colour. When we met it was longer and a honey brown and you were the most effervescent and wild and crazy and most wonderful person I'd ever met, and even then I had trouble keeping my lips from yours. It appears, all these years later, that the urge is as strong now as it was then.'

He cupped her chin with his hand and brushed his thumb over her parted lips. If she'd thought she'd been on fire before, his sweet and gentle caress had only enhanced the power surging between them.

'I know I'm being selfish, Reg,' he continued a moment later when she hadn't spoken. 'Especially after the way I treated you all those years ago, and I really need to tell you how sorry I am. I was arrogant and rude and didn't take into consideration that your feelings were much deeper than I'd originally thought.'

'You asked me to marry you, Flynn!' Reggie shook her head and twisted from his embrace. Flynn instantly released her, dropping his arms back to his sides. 'You proposed marriage and I accepted. Then, the next day, you turn up at my room and tell me you need to call it all off. Just like that. No explanation, just that you'd made a mistake and that you were no longer…free to pursue a relationship with me. Less than two weeks later I read—in the society columns—that Flynn Jamieson, of the well-known wealthy Jamieson family and heir to the Jamieson Corporation, had wed his childhood sweetheart, Violet Fleming, a young philanthropic socialite who was on the board of so many charity organisations it was almost impossible for the newspaper to list them.'

'Reg…I—'

'What, Flynn? Please tell me what happened back then because I've spent the past six years trying to figure things out. What did I do wrong? Was I too enthusiastic? Did everything just happen too fast? Sure, I may be spontaneous and, yes, in my life, once I make a decision, things tend to move really fast and I'm off like a rocket, but what a lot of people don't realise is that I think about things far more deeply than anyone would ever guess, and when you proposed to me I didn't take it lightly or as some sort of flippant twenty-four-hour whimsy.' She shook her head and spread her arms wide.

'I'm just not sure how you could have misconstrued my true feelings for you, especially as when you proposed I threw my arms around your neck and smothered your face in kisses while saying "Yes, yes and yes" over and over again! Don't you think that during the time we were together I hadn't dreamed of you asking me that question? That I didn't feel that strong and abiding connection that—stupid me—I thought you'd felt, too...or at least I believed you when you said you did.'

'Reg!'

'What?' Reggie leaned her head against Bergan's office door, wishing she had her pass key on her so they could at least enter and have a bit of privacy. She was tired and edgy after the retrieval, and then having her patient pass away...it was all becoming too much. Now they were just waiting for the young girl to arrive in A and E, in case she required surgery.

It definitely wasn't the time for them to be having *this* discussion, the one she'd wanted to have with him ever since he'd come back into her life—to ask him why he'd really called off their engagement. Apparently time just wasn't on her side at the moment.

'Will you let me get a word in edgeways?'

'Go for it.' She turned and leaned her back against the door, closing her eyes and waiting for him to speak.

He was quiet for a moment before saying softly, 'It was a mistake.'

Reggie was glad she hadn't been looking at him when he'd spoken those words because the pain that instantly pierced her heart, she knew, would have been clearly reflected in her gaze. She tried to focus on the Christmas music playing through the speaker above, hoping that her days really would be merry and bright, but how could they possibly ever be that way again when Flynn had just confirmed that proposing to her had been a mistake?

'Thanks for confirming that,' she returned, realising she needed to get away from him. In some ways it was the last thing she'd expected him to say, to admit that what they'd had in Sint Maarten had been a mistake, but he'd said it to her back then and he was only confirming it now, all these years later.

The sounds of ambulance sirens nearing the hospital could be heard over the Christmas music and the next instant both her and Flynn's pagers started to beep. She dragged in a deep breath, pushed her personal thoughts aside and stepped away from the door.

Raising her gaze to hover just near the top of retrieval suit, focusing on his Adam's apple, she mumbled, 'Looks like we're needed again.'

With that, she edged past him, ignoring the way her body burst with excitement as her arm brushed against his. Retrieval suit or not, the slightest touch from Flynn would no doubt always set her on fire and it was probably something she should simply learn to accept, rather than fight. She was attracted to Flynn. Fact. He thought the two of them together was a mistake. Fact. All of this made it highly plausible that she would no doubt die from a broken heart.

'Clamp,' she instructed the theatre nurse, Susan, as they entered their fourth hour of surgery. The young girl, Lola, had a perforated bladder and kidney and her bowel was in a bit of a state. 'Nothing we can't fix,' she and Flynn had reassured Lola's poor parents.

Working in conjunction with the urological surgical team, as well as Mackenzie and John for Lola's orthopaedic injuries of an amputated right foot, Flynn and Reggie were determined that this young girl would live. Kev had given his life for her and there was no way any of the team was going to do anything but their best for Lola, no matter how tired they might be.

Lola would need to be on dialysis while her kidney healed and then there was the inevitable right-foot prosthesis she would require, but for the moment both Reggie and Flynn were concentrating on performing an ileostomy, having already successfully completed a resection on the large intestine. They'd had to make a large cut down the centre of Lola's belly in order to gain access to the area. Usually the procedure was performed laparoscopically but in Lola's case that hadn't been an option.

Between the dialysis and the prosthesis, Lola would also have to deal with the temporary stoma they'd been forced to insert—where they attached her small intestine to the outer wall of her body. Her stools would need to go through the stoma into a drainage bag outside her body. All of that was a lot for a twelve-year-old to cope with, especially as it would all be combined with the emotional trauma of being swept out with the ocean current into dangerous waters until Kev had come to her rescue.

As Reggie pulled off her gloves quite some time later, handing Lola's care over to Mackenzie and John, who were the next surgeons to treat Lola's plethora of injuries, she was physically and emotionally drained.

'That poor kid,' Flynn murmured, as he de-gowned in the anteroom next to Reggie.

'Her whole life has just changed,' she replied, removing her mask and cap before running her fingers through her hair, fluffing it up.

'It'll never be the same again.' Flynn continued to watch her, both of them now dressed in their scrubs. Bits of Reggie's dark hair stuck out at all angles, making her look cuter than ever. A lopsided smile slowly tugged at the corners of his mouth and, unable to resist the chance to touch her, he stepped forward and brushed his fingers through the locks so they didn't look so wild and unruly. 'Lovely,' he said.

'Tired,' she returned, unable to put her shields up. After what Flynn had said to her before Lola's surgery Reggie had most definitely wanted to put a bit more distance between them but right now all she really wanted was to find a nice, comfortable bed, curl up and go to sleep.

The feel of his fingers in her hair, his hand cupping her cheek, the way he looked down into her upturned face, the way he looked into her eyes for a brief moment before nodding, as though reading her thoughts, was lovely. To have him here, have him near, have him caring for her. It was something she'd dreamed about for such a very long time that when he put his arms around her shoulders and led her out of the anteroom, she was more than happy to let him.

'Get changed. I'll write up the notes and meet you back here in ten minutes. OK?'

'Sounds good,' she murmured, and headed into the female changing rooms. She was at that stage of exhaustion where she had so many thoughts running through her head that none of them made any sense. One thought blurred into another and they all continued to tumble until she was unable to process anything. So much had happened today and as she slowly changed out of her clothes, almost falling over once or twice, feeling light-headed as though she was drunk, all she could think about was getting to that nice, comfortable bed.

'You're starting to make a habit of this,' Flynn murmured not too much later as they headed to his car. There was a light smattering of rain outside but the air was still rather sticky and humid. She knew he was referring to the exhaustion she'd felt last night.... Had it only been last night? She liked it when her days were full, when time didn't drag, but the past few days had been filled with far too many conflicting emotions, even for her.

'I'm sorry if I'm being a nuisance,' Reggie remarked, the balmy weather having woken her up a little, but Flynn instantly dismissed her words.

'You're not. You've been through a lot, Reggie, and your mind needs time to process everything. At least I don't need to carry you to the car tonight.'

Reggie frowned at him. 'Stop talking about me as though you're the authority on me,' she protested as he unlocked his car and opened the door for her. She stepped forward and only realised a split second later that they were standing facing each other with only the car door between them. She lifted her chin, annoyance making her brave.

'Why not?'

'Because you don't know me, Flynn. Because you've admitted to me that you and I were a mistake, one that should never have happened, that you regret—'

'What?' He frowned as he interrupted her. 'I never said that.'

'Yes, you did. Just before Lola's surgery. We were outside Bergan's office and you admitted it was a mistake to—' She stopped talking again but only because Flynn had put his finger across her lips, startling her and causing her body to be flooded with a mass of tingles at the feather-light touch.

'You once told me the only way to effectively shut you up was to kiss you and I'm very close to doing that, Reg.' He breathed out a calming breath but she could see his eyes flashing with a mixture of desire and frustration. 'What I said to you before Lola's surgery was that it was a mistake to have treated you the way I did. It was a mistake to allow myself to be persuaded by my family. It was a mistake to turn and walk away from you.'

Reggie stared at him then blinked one long blink as though she was desperately trying to process his words. 'A mistake to...'

'Walk away from you. I have many regrets, Reg, and...' He cupped her face, the frustration leaving him as he gazed into her eyes as though she really was the most important and precious person in the world to him. Her legs started to quiver, to turn to jelly, and she quickly put out a hand, clutching the edge of the car door in order to steady herself. 'You are perhaps my biggest regret of all.'

'I am?'

His smile was instant and gorgeous and his eyes were twinkling with mild amusement. 'Yes.' Flynn indicated to the car. 'Get in, Reggie. I think it's time we talked.'

She did as he suggested, trying not to fumble with her seat belt as his words reverberated around her head. Time they talked? Talked about what? About the past? About how he'd left? About how she'd been utterly devastated and heartbroken? Because if they did that, then that discussion would lead to the present and she wasn't at all sure she was ready to reveal to Flynn just how incredible he made her feel.

She loved being near him, spending time with him, laughing with him, and it was also what she wanted more than anything in the world...but...had too much already passed between them? Was it possible she could forgive him for hurting her all those years ago? For breaking her heart and leaving her feeling as though she'd been living a lie ever since?

'You must talk about this,' she could well remember Sunainah saying a few months after she had returned from the Caribbean. 'Talk about your love for this man, this Flynn. It is important for you to do.'

'No, it isn't.'

'It is not healthy, Reggie. If you keep it all bottled up inside, then a day will come when you are unable to contain it any longer. It will bubble up and burst everywhere, making an awful mess,' Sunainah had persisted.

'I can cope with this, Sunainah. I've coped with worse. You know about my past. You know the betrayals I've coped with. Flynn's betrayal is just another one to add to the pile.' She'd shrugged then shaken her head.

'It's my own fault, really. I, in all my romantic stupidity, thought Flynn was different. That he was a man who truly cared about me, who meant it when he said he loved me. Turns out he didn't. He's no different from any other rich man. Only out for what he can get.' Even as she'd spoken the words her heart had been pierced with pain, her voice breaking on the last words.

Sunainah had hugged her close and a fresh bout of tears had fallen on her friend's shoulder. 'What will you do?'

'What I always do.' Reggie had sniffed and dabbed at her eyes with a tissue before blowing her nose. 'I'll cry and then box everything up in my mind and shove it into a dark corner. Then I'll pick myself up and rely on my awesome friends to be there for me.'

'We are pretty awesome.' Sunainah had chuckled.

'And I will be as bright and cheerful as I know how. If I fold a facade around me, one I can control, letting people believe I am forever the happy-go-lucky girl, I'll be able to cope.'

'I hope you are correct.'

Reggie had hugged Sunainah close before standing up to pace around the room. 'I will be happy. I'll lock my love for Flynn away and never think about it again.'

'That is impossible.'

'Probably.' She'd stared at a photograph of the two of them together, standing on the beach at sunset, holding big, colourful drinks with little umbrellas in them. 'Goodbye, Flynn,' she'd whispered, then kissed the photograph and handed it to Sunainah. 'Hide this somewhere for me.'

'Are you sure?' Sunainah had asked.

Reggie had closed her eyes, a single tear falling from her lashes before she'd taken a deep, cleansing breath and slowly released it. Then she'd opened her eyes, forced a smile onto her lips and laughed. 'Positive.'

'Is that the answer to my question or your projected attitude?'

'Both.'

And Reggie had done her best to be that happy-go-lucky girl for the past six years, doing her best to redirect her thoughts whenever she'd accidentally caught herself thinking about Flynn, wanting to know what he was up to, where he was working, whether or not he had children with his stunningly gorgeous wife. She'd stopped reading the social pages, turning off the television or radio at any mention of the Jamieson Corporation. She hadn't wanted to know.

She'd focused on her work, an ever-present smile on her face, her bright and cheerful attitude becoming less forced and more of who she really was. And whenever she had slipped for a minute and indulged herself by wondering what the heir to the Jamieson Corporation was doing with his life, she would force herself to go out on a date. There was no shortage of handsome men working at the hospital but none of them had ever been able to break through the walls she'd erected so firmly about her heart.

Then Flynn had appeared, standing across the corridor from her clinic room, and everything had started to crumble. Now he wanted to talk? Now he wanted to set the record straight? He *hadn't* thought the two of them together was a mistake? Was this a world she wanted to enter again? Surely a leopard didn't change its spots. Surely, given that Flynn had hurt her once, he would do it again.

He switched the radio on as they drove through the quiet streets of Maroochydore but where Reggie had wanted nothing more than to sleep before, Flynn's words had been like a shot of adrenaline and she was now very much awake.

He wanted to talk. That could mean anything, so what on earth was he going to say…and was she going to like it?

CHAPTER EIGHT

'ANOTHER LONG DAY,' she murmured as they walked into his town house. She didn't know if she could face this 'talk' with Flynn on top of the day they'd had. Maybe she should just go straight to her room and hide there for as long as she could.

'I'll put the kettle on,' he said. 'Why don't you sit in the lounge and I'll join you in a moment?'

'Actually, Flynn, if you don't mind…' Reggie eased her way through the kitchen, aiming towards the downstairs bedroom. 'Can we talk later?'

'No.'

'But I'm exhausted.'

Flynn looked at her for a long moment before shaking his head. 'No.'

'No?' she questioned, feeling her annoyance beginning to rise. 'You can't make me sit down and talk about something I'm not sure I want to talk—'

Without a word, he moved quickly, gently scooping her into his arms and pressing his mouth to hers in one swift motion, effectively shutting her up, just as he'd warned her earlier. Reggie barely had time to register his movements before a flood of delight and excitement zinged around her body like an out-of-control pinball. He knew how to move his mouth against hers in order to garner a response of pleasure and it appeared he wasn't above using this knowledge and skill right now.

At first, though, he didn't move his mouth, just pressed his lips to hers as though needing to reacquaint himself with her gloriousness, but after breathing her in, after closing his eyes and allowing the drug that was Reggie to once more flow through his system, Flynn eased back ever so marginally and deepened the kiss.

Slowly, slowly, slowly. As though inflicting the most exquisite torture on their senses, he coaxed her lips to part gently, the taste of her fuelling his desire. She was all sweetness and light and sunshine, bringing her unique brand of pleasure back into his life. It was what she'd done all those years ago, breaking down his barriers, wanting him, needing him, teaching him how to lighten up, not to take things so seriously, to be free from repression.

'You're too stuffy,' she'd once told him, and he'd been impressed with the way she'd teased and laughed at him, so unlike any of the other women he'd met throughout his life. Most of them had only wanted one thing—access to his family's fortune.

'Women aren't interested in *you*, son, and they never will be,' his father had told him time and time again. 'All they want are clothes and shoes and jewellery and anything else your money can buy them. Sure, they might show a smidgen of affection for you in the beginning but it'll wane. It always does.'

'So…you and Mum?' Flynn had questioned him. 'What? Mum only married you for your money?'

'Your mother had money of her own, son. That's the point. Marry someone who already has money and you know they don't want you *just* for your money.' His father had dragged heavily on his expensive Cuban cigar, then coughed. 'Even then, they're happy to take whatever you give them. Everyone has their price.'

And yet, when Flynn had met Reggie, he'd had the distinct impression that she really *didn't* have a price at all. All she'd wanted out of life had been to be happy and to spread that happiness to others. She was a clever, caring and charismatic woman who had completely turned his head.

They'd both been staying in the short-term accommodation apartments owned by the hospital to house the doctors who spent time working in Sint Maarten, so they'd bumped into each other quite frequently. Then one night, in the apartment complex's large, almost empty dining room, when Flynn had been sitting alone at a table, Reggie had pulled out the chair opposite him and sat down.

'Well, it seems completely ridiculous for the two of us to be eating by ourselves, especially as you're new here,' she'd offered by way of explanation. Before he'd been able to say a word, the waitress had brought over their meals and he'd found himself eating—and enjoying—dinner with Reggie Smith.

The more time he'd spent with her, the more intrigued he'd become. She was so carefree, crazy and challenging, making him re-evaluate some of his ideals. Soon he'd been unable to stop himself from kissing her and before his time in Sint Maarten had ended, he'd found himself proposing to the most wonderful and exhilarating woman he'd ever known.

Now Flynn gathered her as close as he could, unable to believe he was permitted to hold her once again, to tenderly caress her back, to continue to absorb her delightful response to the kisses he was pressing to her lips. Didn't she have any idea just how perfect she was for him? How he'd wished he hadn't been so spine-less all those years ago and had stood up for what *he'd* wanted instead of continuing to allow his overbearing father to dictate his life?

But that was then and this was now. He'd made the break, he'd taken control over his own life and somehow he'd found his way back to the one place he'd always felt like he belonged—with Reggie's arms wrapped around him, her mouth responding enthusiastically to his.

'Flynn.' She whispered his name as she reluctantly broke her mouth from his, her breathing erratic and un-even. She put both hands on his shoulders and eased back. 'We can't do this again.' She tried to shake her head but instead found her lips once more captured by his. She moaned with delight, wanting his glorious tor-ture to continue forever as well as wanting it to finish as soon as possible so she didn't end up revealing just how much she still cared for him.

She knew she should push him away, to break the contact. Self-preservation was usually high on her list of priorities but this was Flynn and where he was con-cerned she'd never been able to think straight. When they'd first met he'd turned her mind to mush. When they'd argued he'd turned her mind to mush. When he'd smiled at her, hugged her, kissed her, he'd turned her mind to mush.

At first, in Sint Maarten, she'd done her best to keep their relationship strictly professional, wanting to deny the uncharacteristic desire she'd felt towards him. She hadn't dated wealthy men. That had been her one rule and even though Flynn hadn't told her about his exces-sively rich family, from the moment she'd met him she'd known exactly who he was.

She'd appreciated his skills as a doctor, she'd liked

the way they'd seemed to work together so seamlessly, enjoying the inventive ways and solutions he'd devised for dealing with a variety of situations. What she hadn't expected was to find herself wanting to spend more time with him, to talk to him, to tease him, to laugh with him outside working hours.

And then he'd broken her heart, he'd rejected her love and he'd left her. Even though she wanted to see where this frightening natural chemistry that still existed between them might lead, she wasn't sure her heart was strong enough to endure another rejection from him. As the pain from her past, the pain she'd locked away so tightly, started to bubble up and over, she felt a surge of power course through her and pushed her hands against his shoulders.

'No!' She broke from his embrace and took a step away, bumping into the wall and almost tripping over. Flynn instinctively reached out a hand towards her, wanting to help her, but she shifted farther away.

'Reggie?'

As she looked at him, she was pleased to see he was equally as out of breath, as shaken up with repressed desire as she was. It was nice to know she wasn't the only one affected by the raw, animalistic power that still existed between them.

'I can't do this, Flynn.'

'Do…what?'

'This!' She indicated the distance between them, the thick, heavy attraction that was surrounding them, wanting to draw them closer.

'Why? What is it that's stopping you?'

She stared at him with incredulity. 'Er…how about the fact that you broke my heart?' She turned to walk away, not wanting to relive the pain and mortification he'd inflicted on her. She'd been very disciplined *not* to think about it and she wasn't about to start now, especially *not* in front of him.

Flynn nodded. 'If it's any consolation, I broke mine as well.'

That stopped her. Frowning, she turned to face him. 'What?'

'As I said before at the car, walking away from you that night was not only the hardest thing I've ever done but also the stupidest.'

'Stupidest?'

Flynn raked a hand through his hair, his agitation quite evident. 'I was a fool, Reggie, and for years I've wanted to humbly beg your forgiveness. Now that you're here, in front of me, willing to listen to me, that's exactly what I'm doing.' He looked into her eyes. 'Will you? Can you...forgive me?'

Reggie stared at him in utter astonishment. 'But... wait a second. If breaking up with me broke your heart as well, why did you do it?' She spread her arms wide, her eyes revealing just how perplexed she was with what he was saying.

'My parents.' He shook his head. 'Pressure from my father, emotional blackmail from my mother.' He raked a hand through his hair. 'All my life I'd been told that women would never be interested in *me* for *me*. That when they looked at me all they would see was a walking chequebook. Money would always win out against love, or so I'd been led to believe. But the other fact was that my mother was very ill back then, and there was some controversy as to whether I should even go to the Caribbean in the first place. Although I haven't necessarily seen eye to eye with my parents over the years, they're still my parents and I'm honour bound to them.'

Reggie snorted at his words. '"Honour bound". Ha. What honour? The world of the wealthy. It has its own way to bully and oppress.'

'Er…yes.' He seemed astonished she understood.

'I take it her health improved as you did indeed come to the Caribbean.'

'Yes, and while I was there, while I was with *you*, I started to see the world differently. *You* helped me to see it differently and I started to realise the world I'd been raised in had certain…flaws.'

'One being that it was OK to think for yourself?'

'Yes.' Again he was surprised at her insight.

'And the marriage you entered into the instant you left me?'

'It was my mother's final wish.'

'Let me guess. Your mother was good friends with Violet's mother?'

'The best of friends, yes.'

Reggie shrugged and turned away from him, walking into the lounge room and slumping down into a chair, closing her eyes.

'As ridiculous and as old-fashioned as it might sound, our mothers had always talked of Violet and I marrying, all our lives. We were to have children who would bind our two families together forever.'

'And how did you and Violet feel about this?'

Flynn shrugged. 'Violet was more like a sister to me. Neither of us have siblings. As far as the arranged marriage went, I guess as I'd always been told that was what was expected of me, I didn't think about it much. Until…until I met you.'

'You were OK with having an arranged marriage?'

'Back then, I guess I was…but as I've said, then I met you and everything changed.'

'But the wealthy are supposed to marry the wealthy.' She shook her head, looking at him through her lashes. 'It's snobbish and elitist and not to mention outdated.'

'And yet it's still happening even today.' Flynn sat down on the lounge next to her, facing her, needing her to understand. 'My mother's health deteriorated while I was in Sint Maarten but I didn't know that as I hadn't been answering their calls. I'd wanted to shut out my life, ignore the pressures waiting for me once I returned to Melbourne. I wanted to live in the world you and I had created for ourselves, to stay happy in our bubble.'

'And when you finally reconnected with that world?'

'I was told my mother had been admitted to hospital only a few hours before. Guilt swamped me, especially when my father continued to lecture me about my irresponsible behaviour of not staying in contact. And there I was, calling them to tell them the good news, to let them know that I'd found the woman of my dreams and that I was engaged.

'When I told my father that I'd most certainly come home but that I was bringing my new fiancée with me, he told me I might as well stick a scalpel directly into my mother's heart and kill her instantly. He blustered about how the wedding to Violet was set. That it was my mother's final wish to see Violet and I married and that was what was going to happen.

'He talked to me long and hard about my duty, my honour, my need to step up and do the right thing. He convinced me that there was no way any woman— *you*—could ever feel anything deep and abiding for me, nothing that would stand the test of time.'

Flynn closed his eyes and shook his head. 'He'd sent his private jet to the airport for me and I was to be on it the following afternoon. Alone. I was so eaten up with guilt. My mother had been ill and I'd been selfish enough to shut her out simply because I'd been with you.

'I paced around, thinking things through, trying to rationalise whether or not you truly loved me, and yet somehow...my thinking changed. I did find it difficult to believe that you could really love me for me, that you must know about my family's money and that was the only reason you'd even given me the time of day.'

'You were angry with me.' Reggie's statement was soft but clear. 'I could see it in your eyes.'

He closed his eyes for a moment as though recalling that horrible scene in her room when he'd called off their engagement. 'I was, but only because I'd convinced myself you couldn't possibly love *me*,' he admitted honestly. 'It was easier for me to break it off with you if I believed you'd only been interested in me for my family fortune.'

'The wealthy can behave however they like and nine times out of ten they do. A law unto themselves.'

Flynn looked at her with a hint of surprise. 'I disagree with that statement, at least as far as I'm concerned.'

'Perhaps now, but not back then. Your father dictated your path and you just let him. You let his voice get into your head and control you, just as it always had.'

'I know, but...' Flynn shifted in his seat, defence at her attack on his father grating on him, even though he knew what she was saying was absolutely true. 'My mother was ill. *Gravely* ill. She passed away five days after the wedding.'

'And was she happy?'

'Seeing me married to Violet? Yes, she was. It was what happened after that which I didn't appreciate.'

'Being stuck in an arranged marriage?' she guessed.

'Well, there was that, but, more importantly, not three days after my mother's funeral my father threw a large wedding reception, inviting everyone who *should* have been invited to what he termed was "the society wedding of the year".' Flynn waved his hand in the air as though he was announcing a headline.

'Did you know about it?'

'Of course.'

'And you couldn't stop it?'

'I wanted to but everyone kept saying it was what Mum had wanted, that she'd helped to plan it and that if it didn't go ahead, we were dishonouring her memory.'

'And there's more guilt piled on.'

'Exactly.' Flynn reached over and took Reggie's hand in his. 'I was also highly conscious of you. I kept wondering what you must be thinking.' He looked down at her fingers, stroking them lightly. 'I knew you probably hated me and I wouldn't have blamed you for the atrocious way I'd behaved. You didn't know that because of my social status, because of my family's wealth, my picture would be splashed around on every glossy magazine in Australia.'

'Actually...' she nodded '...I did know about your wealth.'

He angled his head to the side, frowning a little. 'You mean after I left the Caribbean?'

'No. I knew exactly who you were from the moment we met.'

'What?'

'I knew you were the heir apparent to the Jamieson Corporation.'

'You did?' He looked down at her hand again, before meeting her eyes. 'That wasn't why you...?'

He trailed off, feeling stupid for even voicing the

thought, but suddenly he recalled his father's bitter words, the doubts that he had placed in Flynn's head once upon a time. Caught up in the grief of losing his mother, breaking things off with Reggie and being pressured to marry a woman who was more a sister than a wife, Flynn's temper had exploded when his father had refused to back down about the wedding reception.

'If you go ahead with this, I will not attend,' he'd told his father.

'Don't be ridiculous, Flynn. Of course you'll be there.'

'No. I've only just buried my mother and I want time to grieve before we go splashing our fake happiness around the society pages.'

'Fake happiness! Violet is a fine woman and she'll make you a fine wife. She's perfect for you, Flynn. She always has been.'

'I think Violet might have something to say about that.'

'Violet does whatever she's told. She doesn't have an original thought in her head. She's been told her whole life that she's going to marry you and she's accepted it.'

'Then she's wrong.' Flynn had shaken his head. 'I love someone else, Dad.' There. The words had finally been spoken and where Flynn had somehow thought they would make a difference, his father had flicked the statement aside with a wave of his hand as though he had been shooing away a pesky fly.

'What do you know about love? Some gold-digging nurse you met in the Caribbean? A holiday romance? That's not serious, Flynn. All women see when they look at you is dollar signs. They want your money, not you. That's where Violet is different. She comes from money.'

'And the fact that you and her father are merging your businesses has nothing at all to do with this.'

His father had spread his hands wide as though indicating he had nothing to hide. 'Just seizing an opportunity, son.'

'Sure.' Flynn had stalked to the window and looked out at the extensive grounds. So green when everywhere else in the country had been brown due to drought. 'She wasn't a nurse and she wasn't a gold-digger.' He'd spoken the words more to himself than to his father, needing to reassure himself of the real reasons Reggie had admitted to loving him.

'You think that, if it helps you sleep at night but, rest assured, if she knew you had money, that would be the only reason she latched onto you.' His father had tapped his own chest. 'I've just saved the company tens of thousands of dollars in settlement fees, not to mention protecting us from having our private affairs splashed all over the papers.'

'Oh, but splashing this wedding reception all over the papers is fine?'

'It's controlled. Now, go and find Violet and thank your lucky stars you had a mother who was looking out for your best interests by finding you the right wife.'

Flynn exhaled slowly as he ran his fingers over Reggie's hand once more, marvelling at her soft, silky skin. These were the hands that had performed intricate surgery on twelve-year-old Lola, the hands that had held his as they'd walked along the beach, the hands that had caressed his face before she'd whispered the words 'I love you' near his lips.

'Are you trying to ask me if I fell in love with you because of your *money*?' She all but spat the word at him.

'Er…um…'

'You don't sound too sure about that, Flynn.' Reggie pulled her hand from his and stood from the lounge, pacing up and down. 'Do you know, it was *because* I knew you came from money that I tried to keep my distance, tried to keep the relationship between us strictly professional.'

'You hugged me on my first day as a way of greeting. That wasn't keeping a distance, Reg,' he stated.

Reggie shrugged. 'That's how I greeted everyone. I didn't want to call attention to the fact that I knew who you were by doing anything different.'

'So you didn't love me?' Flynn felt compelled to asked as he watched her. It was difficult not to stand and drag her back into his arms because when Reggie got fired up like this, she was more dynamic, more beautiful, more alluring than ever.

'Well, of course I loved you…back then. I did agree to marry you and, contrary to how *you* may do things, when I accept a marriage proposal, it's because I'm in love with the man who's asking.' She glared at him, almost daring him to comment.

'I was in love with you back then, too,' he said. 'But I'd been raised to do my duty to my family and… No.' He shook his head again before standing and walking towards her, his hands open, palms up, indicating he had nothing to hide. She stopped pacing for a moment and looked at him. 'No. No more excuses. I hurt you, Reggie and for that I apologise.'

She gave him a brief nod, showing she accepted his words, and while part of her wanted nothing more than to throw herself into his arms and press her mouth to his, the other part was still simmering with repressed anger. Flynn came from money, from a wealthy and prestigious family, and she knew, firsthand, that those types of people couldn't be trusted. Had he changed? Well, he was divorced from his pretty socialite wife, or so the tabloids had reported a while back, but who was to say that was actually true?

She angled her head, needing to check. 'You *are* divorced from Violet, aren't you?'

'Yes.'

Reggie clenched her jaw and crossed her arms over her chest. 'But you still want to be sure that I didn't chase after you for your money, don't you? You'll always be wondering, right?' When he didn't immediately answer she rolled her eyes and started to pace again.

'Well, you'll be pleased to hear, Flynn, that I have *never* been interested in one single penny of your precious Jamieson Corporation millions. Not then and most definitely not now. Even accepting your help with relocating my neighbours, knowing the big corporation was footing the bill and no doubt using it as a tax dodge, was a big hurdle for me to personally overcome.'

'I didn't offer the corporation's money to help those people, Reg,' he quickly interjected. 'I'm offering my own. The wealth, as you term it, that I have now has nothing to do with my father's corporation. The money I have came to me after my mother's death. My inheritance. I was cut out of my father's will and, therefore, any claim to the corporation the moment I signed the divorce papers.'

That stopped her pacing. She stared at him in surprise. 'You…you've walked away from your father?'

'From his blackmail, from his controlling presence, from his world? Yes.'

'Oh.' She dropped her arms back to her sides. 'I didn't realise.'

'It's been three years now.'

'You've been divorced for three years?'

'Officially, yes.'

'Oh,' she said again, the anger starting to dissipate. 'And you didn't…?' She stopped. How could she possibly ask him if he'd thought of her during that time? Whether he'd tried to find her? Had he even really cared about her amidst all his other family politics?

'Didn't what?' he prompted, but she shook her head and thankfully he dropped the subject. Flynn took a tentative step towards her and when she didn't back away he tried another and another until he was standing before her. 'It was a mistake for me to marry Violet.'

'Yes.'

'It was a mistake for me to treat you so badly.'

'Yes.'

Flynn reached out and brushed his fingers through her gorgeous black locks. 'Do you think we can try again?'

'Try again…as in…what? What does that mean?'

'It means…' he reached down and linked his free hand with hers '…that we see if, after everything we've been through, whether we're still…compatible.' His tone was soft, smooth and inviting. Reggie could feel herself beginning to crumble, could feel the walls she so desperately wanted to keep in place begin to weaken, and when he bent his head and brushed a soft and tantalising kiss across her cheek, her eyelids fluttered closed and she breathed in the scent of him.

Good heavens. The man smelled fantastic. How did he do that after such a busy and stressful day?

'I don't…' She stopped and swallowed over the dryness of her throat. 'I don't know, Flynn.'

'Why? Because I hurt you before?' He brushed a kiss to her other cheek, lingering a little longer.

'Mmm-hmm,' she sighed, parting her lips to allow the pent-up air to escape.

'Do you think you can trust me again?' He whispered the words near her mouth, keeping such a marginal distance that she started to yearn for his lips to be on hers once more. From their very first kiss to their very last, his mouth had always fitted hers perfectly, as though they'd been made for each other. 'Do you?'

'I don't know.' The whispered words were barely audible and Flynn drew back slightly. He cupped her face with one hand and brushed his thumb over her parted lips. She gasped with surprised delight, opening her eyes to stare into his. 'The attraction is clearly alive and well.'

'Yes.'

'And I know you trust me as far as work is concerned.'

'Yes.'

'And you know I'd never force you to do anything you didn't want to so I can safely say that you can trust me with your honour.'

'Yes.'

'So what is it, Reggie? What is it that is holding you back from giving me…giving *us* another chance?'

Reggie bit her lip, the intrusive thoughts from her past bursting forth into her mind at his question. Why couldn't she give him another chance? 'Because you're wealthy and I don't trust wealthy people.'

'What?' He eased back, dropping his hand to her shoulder. 'I don't understand.'

'Wealth corrupts. Even the nicest, strongest people. It corrupts them.'

'And you know this how? Because of me being unable to stand up to my father all those years ago?'

'No. This has nothing to do with you, Flynn. It does, however, have everything to do with me.'

'You? You've been hurt by wealthy people before?'

Reggie couldn't believe the way her repressed memories, ones she'd carefully locked away in a mental box with 'Do Not Touch' written all over it, continued to flood her mind. Her anxiety and agitation started to increase and she turned away from Flynn, needing distance, needing space. She sucked in a breath and then another one, trying not to hyperventilate while she desperately searched for her self-control. She breathed out, unable to believe the fear rising within her, making her throat go dry, almost choking her. Flynn frowned, noting the paleness of her complexion.

'Reg?' She could hear the concern in his voice.

She closed her eyes and shook her head, knowing she needed to say these words to Flynn. It was true that she would love to have another chance with him and where all those years ago she'd been unable to talk about her past, unable to open up to him and tell him the disgusting things that had happened to her, she knew if there was ever any hope of any sort of future for herself and Flynn, she had to tell him the truth.

'I can't say it.' The words were a whisper and when he crossed to her and put his hands on her shoulders, coaxing her to look at him, all she could do was close her eyes and shake her head vehemently.

'It's all right, Reggie. Whatever you have to say, I'm here.' He'd never seen her like this before, so small and childlike. The Reggie he'd always known had been larger than life, vibrant, funny, with the most infectious laugh. 'You're starting to really worry me,' he said, and it was then, when she heard the tremor in his voice, that she knew she had to do this.

She swallowed again and opened her eyes. As she lifted her chin so she could meet Flynn's gaze, her heart was pounding furiously in her chest.

'Easy. Gently. It's all right, Reg. I'm here. Right here. Nothing you can say will change that.'

'You haven't heard what it is I have to say.'

'Trust me, Reg.' He brushed a feather-light kiss across her lips, not to break the mood or for any romantic reason but rather to give her courage. 'Please?'

Reggie breathed out again and nodded, his hands on her shoulders helping to calm her anxious brain. 'OK.' She breathed out, unable to believe she was really going to open that hateful box and expose herself, her inner self, to Flynn.

'All those years ago, when we first met, I knew who you were because I was raised in Melbourne, not far from where you lived.'

'What?' It had clearly been the last thing he'd expected her to say.

'I hate wealthy people because…my parents were wealthy. In fact, my father knew your father.'

'What?' She'd clearly stunned him.

'When I turned eighteen I changed my name by deed poll to Regina Smith.'

'Why?' Flynn was starting to get a bad feeling in his stomach at what she was saying. 'What name were you christened with?'

She forced calmness into her words as she spoke. 'My name was…Regina Anne Catherine Elizabeth Fox-Wallington.'

'Fox-Wallington?' He whispered the surname with incredulity and disbelief.

'I see you remember my family well.'

'You're *that* Regina? The young girl who was abused by her parents?'

She forced herself to keep her chin up, to keep looking into his eyes, seeing his own disbelief at what she was saying. 'Yes,' she confirmed. 'I'm *that* Regina.'

CHAPTER NINE

'OH, REG.' FLYNN shook his head, anguish in his voice. 'I remember. It was in the papers, on the news. They'd been abusing you for years. Physically as well as emotionally.'

Strangely enough, now that she'd come this far, now that she'd confessed the secret of her real identity to Flynn, the pressure of the anxiety started to dissipate. She cleared her throat, amazed at how normal her voice sounded when she spoke. 'For years my parents made sure their private physician looked after me, treating my wounds, isolating me when they took longer to heal than expected.'

'What?'

'Wealth corrupts. That doctor had no problem with being paid off and when the truth finally came out, he had the gall to state that he would often suggest they send me to another boarding school in order to save me from their wrath. I was nothing but a punching bag to my father and my mother would slap me around and then put her cigarettes out on me. The physician was struck off the register and is doing gaol time.'

'Oh, Reg.' Tears came into Flynn's eyes as she recounted the events with little to no emotion. It was a defence mechanism, he knew that, but, still, the traumas she must have endured. 'How did you finally managed to bring it all to light?'

'The last school they sent me to, when I was sixteen, was rife with bullies and, quite frankly, by then I'd had enough of being everyone's punching bag. I'd tried to talk to my teachers at school, to counsellors, but no one would ever believe that the great and powerful Walter Fox-Wallington would ever hit his own child.

'As I was treated by their private doctor, there were no medical records of my injuries, of my broken bones, of my extensive bruising—no *proof*—so why *would* anyone believe me? As far as the teachers and counsellors were concerned, I was a spoiled and wealthy brat who was clearly troubled and who loved to make up stories about her parents.

'Besides, if they actually did find the courage to question my parents, which a few of them did, my father would pull his financial support from the school or slap a law suit on anyone who dared question his word.' Reggie shrugged both her shoulders, Flynn's hands rising and falling with the action. 'You can do anything with money. At least, that was my father's motto and one he used to spit at me every time he "donated" enormous sums of money in order to keep people quiet.'

'But surely someone knew he was corrupt?'

'I'm sure plenty of people did but blackmail, self-preservation and the power of wealth go a long way to buying silence. Besides, he'd simply smile brightly and tell people I was a delusional teenager, a spoiled brat with a grudge against her parents.'

'So…how did you…escape that life?' He was agog at what she was saying.

'I ran away from boarding school. I stowed away on a goods train and ended up in Sydney. There, I found a drop-in centre and a solicitor, Elika, who wasn't afraid to take the case on. Pro bono, of course.'

Flynn was still stunned as he stared down into her face. She'd been through so much and his heart ached for her. No wonder she hated people with money. She had good reason to. 'I remember the story breaking.' His words were soft. 'I remember my father doing everything he could to distance himself from the Fox-Wallington fiasco, as he termed it. He also pulled any and all investments he had in your father's companies.'

'So he wasn't as much concerned with what had happened but rather with protecting himself.'

Flynn shrugged. 'Everything was business to him. Even my mother and myself, although my mother knew what sort of life she was signing up for when she married him.'

'The wealthy have their own set of rules and heaven help anyone who dares to stand up to them or go against them.'

'Ain't that the truth.' His words were filled with heartfelt honesty and as Reggie looked into his eyes she saw that perhaps, just perhaps, there was a possibility that Flynn really understood what it was she was trying to say.

'So where are your parents now? I can't remember what happened.'

'They're dead.' The words were said with no emotion, no relief, no bitterness, no pain. 'When my father realised he couldn't buy off the solicitor, he and my mother left the country for Spain.'

Flynn rolled his eyes. 'No extradition.'

'Exactly. They lived there for almost two years, in perfect luxury, before dying in a boating accident.' She frowned, her voice dropping just a little. 'I wasn't sad when I was told of their deaths. Instead, I demanded to see the bodies—just to make sure.'

'You did? It wasn't…traumatic?'

'I'd just started medical school, so I'd seen my fair share of cadavers. Besides, I'm not meaning to sound callous but I needed to know if it was true. To help me come to terms with the horrific things they did to me, I needed to see their cold, dead bodies on that slab.' She looked away from him. 'I'm sorry if that sounds harsh but—'

'I understand, Reg. Those people weren't your parents, they were the monsters who had made your life a misery.'

Reggie jerked her head up in surprise. 'Yes. Exactly.'

'You had to be sure it was really over.'

'And it was. I identified their bodies and with Elika's help organised for their cremations. There was no funeral, no wake, no chance for people to "honour" those monsters.'

Flynn rubbed his hands along her shoulders, knowing he shouldn't be at all surprised at the inner strength this woman possessed. He gazed down into her eyes. 'You are incredible, Reg. So strong and always so happy and bubbly and yet you've been through so much pain. How did you cope?'

'Well, for a start, I found some wonderful friends at medical school. Sunainah, Bergan and Mackenzie have all been through their own pain and anguish and somehow, although the four of us are incredibly different, we bonded because we all understood what it was like to be a victim.'

'And it's a friendship that's as strong and as true over twenty years later.'

'Yes.' She smiled, thinking of the way she and her

friends had stuck together through thick and thin…and how they'd all managed to find the man of their dreams, that one special person they could always rely on, no matter what. The smile started to slide from her lips as she gazed up at Flynn. Was *he* her one special person? The one she could rely on, no matter what?

She'd thought so once before but he'd let her down. Was it possible she could take a chance again? Put her heart out there? Would Flynn hurt her again, especially now that he knew the truth about her past? He was look-ing at her as though she was the most wonderful, most special and most precious person in the world to him. Was that real?

He'd mentioned the attraction between them being still as strong…possibly stronger than before and he'd been right. When he put his arms around her, she felt as though she'd come home. When he kissed her, she felt as though her entire world was filled with sparkles and rainbows and pure happiness. When he gazed down into her eyes, as he was doing right now, her heart con-stricted and her breathing became shallow, wanting him to look at her that way always, to support her always, to love her always.

Could they try again?

'Reg, you are special to me. I hope you believe that.'

'I want to,' she whispered.

'Then do it.' He cupped her face and smiled at her before dipping his head to brush his lips lightly across hers. Reggie closed her eyes, wanting to absorb every sensation he was evoking within her, wanting to lose herself in the pleasure and happiness only Flynn could give her. They'd been so good together all those years ago. Perhaps now they could be better. She parted her lips to deepen the kiss but Flynn edged back. 'Reggie?'

'Mmm?' she sighed, her eyes still closed.

'There's just one thing I need to know.' There was a tentativeness in his tone and she immediately looked at him, worry piercing her.

'What?' She searched his beautiful blue eyes and instinctively realised what it was he was still confused about. 'The money?'

'Yes. Your father, from what I can recall, was worth a lot of money.'

'He was. He left it all to my mother, expecting her to outlive him. She, however, hadn't made a will and as their daughter I inherited it all.'

'You did?'

'I did.'

'So…you're wealthy?'

She shook her head. 'No. I didn't want a penny. I signed the entire fortune over to Elika, the solicitor who helped me, the one person who I knew was unlikely to be corrupted. Then I changed my name. My past was gone. Erased. I had a clean slate and I could start again.'

'Wait.' He eased back and held up one hand. 'Let me get this straight. You gave the *entire* Fox-Wallington fortune away?'

'Yes.'

'But that would have been…billions.'

'Wealth corrupts.' She tried to edge away from him but he immediately put both his hands on her shoulders again.

'But what about medical school?'

'What about it? I did what normal people do. I accepted government funding to pay my university fees, found a cheap place to live and worked all sorts of jobs in order to have enough money to eat.'

'And this solicitor, Elika, what has she done with all that money?'

'Ever heard of the Moffat Drop-in Centres?'

'For teens and abused children?'

'Yes, as well as children and teenagers living on the street, or those who are having a hard time. There's a centre here in Maroochydore that Bergan and Richard do a lot of work with.'

'That's you?'

'No. That's Elika, the solicitor. Well, she's more of a businesswoman nowadays and well into her sixties, but she's still making a difference and the drop-in centres are just the tip of the iceberg. She works with various organisations both in Australia and overseas to help people in need.'

'You just gave all that money away?'

'Why wouldn't I? As far as I was concerned, it was blood money and, besides, it had never brought me happiness. All I've ever wanted was to be normal. A normal girl, doing a normal job, living a normal life.'

'Wow.' He shook his head in wonderment.

'What?'

'You're…so strong.'

'It took me years to piece myself back together, to figure out who I wanted to be as an adult, and with the help of my friends I think I've done a pretty good job.'

'Why didn't you tell me any of this all those years ago?'

'Because it's also taken me years to learn who to trust. It's not an easy thing for me to do and, for the record, I had planned to tell you everything the day after we became engaged, but—'

'But I broke it off.' He closed his eyes, unable to believe how ridiculously stupid he'd been back then.

'And I turned out to be yet another wealthy person you couldn't trust.'

'That's how I saw it.'

'But, for the record, Reggie—and I'm not trying to defend my actions back then or justify my behaviour—I wasn't corrupted by money. I was corrupted by guilt. I didn't marry Violet because my father threatened to cut me off without a cent. I did it because my mother was dying and it was the one thing that would make her happy, to see her son happily settled.'

Reggie looked up into his eyes and for the first time since they'd been talking reached up and brushed her fingers across his cheek. 'You loved your mother.' It was a statement because she could see clearly in his eyes, hear it in his voice.

'I did. Very much.'

'You wanted to make her happy in her last days.'

'Yes, but I let myself get pressured into doing something I should never have done. I resent that now.'

'But you're not that man anymore. I can tell. You're stronger now. You're more...*you*.' She shook her head. 'I'm not explaining that well.'

'No. You're right. I am different.' He gave her a cute, lopsided smile. 'Perhaps these six years apart haven't been a total waste of time.'

'Perhaps we both needed to do some more growing up.'

'Exactly. I've found the courage to change, not because anyone's told me to but because I needed to, for myself. I needed to find out who I was, without my parents, without Violet and without any other pressure.'

'And have you?'

The smile on his lips increased as he shifted towards her, his arms coming about her waist to draw her near.

'Yes. It took me a while to realise it, that I needed to change my life because I wasn't happy.'

'It can be the most difficult thing in the world to do, to take a stand and follow your heart, to do what you know is right.'

'Yes.' He smiled at her. 'And now I need to do what I know is right, to follow my heart and kiss you once more, Reg.'

Reggie loved hearing those words from his mouth and as she sighed against him she couldn't help but raise one teasing eyebrow. 'Only once more?'

His grin widened as he settled her into his arms. 'I like the way you're thinking.' And with that he lowered his head and claimed her mouth in a kiss filled with passion and promise. Exactly what those promises might be she had no idea, but for now she was more than happy just to go with the fact that she'd managed to work up the courage to tell Flynn about her past... and he hadn't rejected her. He'd understood. He'd supported her. He'd accepted.

He was also doing the most wonderful and delectable things to her mouth, tantalising and teasing her senses. The love she knew had never died welled up in her heart, bursting forth with delight throughout her entire body. She loved Flynn. She always had but she knew of old that to love someone didn't necessarily mean there would be a happy ending.

Still, he knew just how to hold her, just how to kiss her, just how to drive her completely crazy with longing. He knew that rubbing small circles at the base of her spine caused tingles to explode within her. He knew that pressing sweet butterfly kisses along her cheek, towards her ear and then down to her neck made goosebumps break out over her entire body.

He knew that whispering words of delight, telling her just how attractive he found her, how he was drawn to her, how he couldn't get enough of her, all drove her almost to distraction.

Soon she was light-headed and swooning, leaning against him for support as her knees started to give way. Within another second Flynn had scooped her up into his arms and carried her to the lounge. He sat down, settling her in his lap, his arms shifting to hold her tightly, his mouth not leaving hers for an instant.

Reggie sighed against him, unable to believe she was finally back here again, back in his arms, back where she'd yearned to be for so very long. Flynn was here. *Her* Flynn, and he was kissing her exactly as he had during all her dreams about him.

'Mmm,' she moaned as he continued to wreak havoc with her senses. She could feel his restraint, feel he was trying to keep things soft and steady, not wanting to scare her away, but didn't he realise that she didn't scare easily? She wanted him. Couldn't he feel that?

The fact that he was taking things slowly was only making her desire for him increase and when he eased his mouth from hers to trace her lips tantalisingly with his tongue, knowing how the action drove her crazy, his breath mingling and blending with hers, Reggie thought her heart would burst.

'Flynn,' she breathed. 'I want you.'

'I know.' He kissed her cheek.

'This can't be wrong. Not a second time.'

'No.' He kissed her other cheek.

'Shouldn't we go…somewhere a little more comfortable?' The words were a husky whisper as he continued to kiss her neck, Reggie tilting her head to the side to grant him all the access he desired.

'No.'

Reggie's eyes flew open, his one-word answer like a stylus scratching its way across a record. 'No?'

'No,' he repeated, his voice thick with repressed desire.

She shifted so she could look at him better and as she did so he seemed to take it as a sign to remove her from his lap and to settle her next to him on the lounge. 'Flynn?' She swallowed over the confusion even she could hear in her voice.

'Reg, I don't want to rush things.' He bent and kissed her lips as though needing her to know he was still very much on board with what was happening between them. 'This time we need to take things slowly.'

'Because we didn't take things slowly last time?'

'Exactly. And…' he brushed the backs of his fingers across her cheek and then pushed some of her dark, spiky locks behind her ear '…you deserve better. With everything you've confessed to me, plus with everything that's happened in the past few days, I think we're definitely starting to move way too fast again. Don't you?'

Reggie stared at him, unable to believe the words were coming out of his mouth. How was it possible he could be even more wonderful, more considerate, more chivalrous than she remembered? He cared about her. He *really* cared about her and he was willing to prove that by slowing things down. She opened her mouth to agree with him but found the words were stuck behind the bubble of emotion, so she nodded instead.

'I was wondering, just this morning, how you were able to deal with your home burning down so easily, how you could just accept the fact and not wallow and cry and scream, as you most certainly have every right to do, but now...' Flynn brushed his thumb over her lips before bending and mimicking the same action with his lips '...with everything you've been through, you've built up an amazing resilience to things beyond your control. That, my beautiful Reg, is an amazing quality and you have it in spades. You just pick yourself up and keep on moving forward and I want you to know just how much I admire you.'

'Oh, Flynn.' She couldn't believe he was saying such nice things to her and quickly fanned her face with her hand, needing to lighten the atmosphere around them with a touch of humour. It worked because he smiled warmly in response. 'You say the sweetest things.'

'I meant every word.'

She dropped the pretence for a moment and nodded. 'I don't doubt it.'

'Good, because I think the next thing we should discuss is getting some sleep—me upstairs, you downstairs and, no, that isn't a euphemism or meant as a *double entendre.*'

Reggie laughed; the sound lighter and freer than she could ever remember hearing before. Flynn removed his arm from around her shoulders, then stood and pulled her to her feet. He held her hand as he walked her to her room. 'Make free use of the bathroom. I'll use the en suite.'

'OK.' She stood at the door to her room and looked up at him. She smiled then stood on tiptoe and kissed him. 'Who said chivalry was dead?' she asked rhetorically.

'Taking things slower is a good thing.'

'Yes.'

'We deserve the time to really get to know each other again.'

'Yes.'

Flynn smiled and took her hand in his, raising it to his lips. 'Sleep sweet, Reg.' Then he bowed from the waist and headed up the stairs, blowing her one last kiss from the top. Reggie couldn't help but giggle as she entered the room, sighing romantically.

'Oh, Flynn, you really do know how to make a girl feel special,' she whispered, and it was so true. She could trust him. He was showing her that by not rushing into things. He cared about her and it was still a little difficult for her to get her head around that realisation. Was it possible that this time they'd be able to really move forward with their life together? A normal life together? After all, wasn't Flynn the most perfect man for her?

Surely, with everything they'd discussed tonight, there was no way he'd ever hurt her again. Right?

CHAPTER TEN

FROM THE NEXT morning, even though they hadn't specifically discussed it, they appeared to be back together. When Reggie had come into the kitchen for breakfast, Flynn once more having already made the coffee and toast, he'd crossed to her side, given her a hug and brushed a light kiss across her lips.

'Good morning,' he'd said, smiling warmly at her.

'Morning,' she'd returned, before hugging him back, unable to believe how wonderful it felt to be so familiar with him again. He drove them to the hospital but still kept his distance in front of their colleagues, which she was happy about because she wasn't ready for everyone to be staring and gawking at them when she was still trying to figure things out.

He took her shopping for clothes and shoes and all the other little things she needed, not appearing bored by any of the shops they visited or insisting she shop at the most expensive places. She modelled clothes for him, twirling and laughing and smiling and trying to remember when she'd last been this happy. Her car was returned from the garage and he insisted she leave it in his garage, parking his own car in the driveway.

The little girl, Lola, who had been attacked by the shark, was starting to make progress with her recovery and while it would indeed be a long journey, all the surgeons involved in her care were happy with the way her body was coping with the trauma.

Things were also building up for the hospital's Christmas auction and Reggie and Mackenzie spent quite a bit of time finalising the details.

'One of the outpatient ward clerks signed me up for the bachelor auction that very first morning I was in Outpatients,' Flynn told Reggie when she noticed his name on the sign-up sheet.

'But you're not a bachelor anymore,' she felt compelled to point out.

'Well, technically I am as I'm not married.'

'But we are in a…relationship…' She looked at him with concern. 'Aren't we?'

Or did he just think their time together was a fling? Something to keep him occupied during his six months at the hospital? Had she grasped the wrong end of the stick again? Did she feel more for him than he felt—

'Stop,' he commanded, and when she looked at him, her eyes wide with concern and worry, she noticed he was smiling at her, slowly shaking his head from side to side. 'I can hear your thoughts from here, Reg.' He cupped her face and brought his lips down to warm hers. 'Of course we're in a relationship. Together. Both of us. Mutually exclusive. But apart from our closest friends, no one at the hospital knows that. To pull out of the auction now would raise suspicion.'

'And you don't want to do that?'

Flynn tugged her into his arms, nuzzling her neck once more. 'I like having you all to myself, Reg. I like not having people gossip about us as we walk by. During our lives, and for different reasons, we've both been the topic of discussion and while I know it will happen one day, that the cat will be out of the proverbial bag, I just want a bit longer to have you all to myself.' He pressed his mouth to hers, making her swoon with delight from his glorious kisses.

'I guess it is for a good cause,' she rationalised.

'And I'm absolutely positive that there's a very special woman who's going to ensure she wins the auction.' He glared pointedly at her.

'Really? Which woman is that?' Reggie giggled but pretended to ponder the question. 'Ingrid Brown? She's very interested in you.'

He wrinkled his nose. 'A great surgical registrar but not my type.'

'Clara from Outpatients? Or perhaps—' Her words were cut off as Flynn kissed her into silence.

'You are going to win that auction, Reg,' he whispered in her ear after tantalising her with a thread of butterfly kisses, a spate of delighted goose-bumps flooding her skin. 'Even if I have to give you every last cent.' He lifted his head and looked into her eyes. 'I don't want to be with any other woman—except you.'

Reggie sighed into him as his wonderful words penetrated her heart, accepting the way his mouth continued to create havoc with her equilibrium.

She was still walking on feathers, on pillows, on air when she met Bergan, Mackenzie and Sunainah for coffee. Christmas wasn't that far away and everywhere she went there were people collecting for charity, Santa Clauses in every store, tinsel, carollers and a generally festive atmosphere that was difficult to ignore.

'So…you and Flynn? Still super-happy?' Mackenzie asked.

'Do you even need to ask? Just look at her,' Bergan

pointed out. 'It's as plain as the nose on your face,' she remarked, before sipping her coffee.

'You are even happier than usual,' Sunainah added.

'And this time,' Mackenzie remarked as she grinned widely at her friend, 'the happiness you're shining out at the world isn't forced—it's real.'

Reggie giggled, nodding her head at the three of them. 'It's so wonderful and exciting and new and scary and—'

'We've all been there.' Bergan's tone was matter-of-fact. 'A mixture of emotions that keeps your insides churning with angst and delight. You don't need to go on about it.' She wasn't usually one for gushy senti-mentality but she reached over and pressed a kiss to her friend's cheek. 'And I couldn't be happier for you,' she said softly, and all of them laughed.

'So are there any plans for a wed—?'

'Stop!' Reggie held up her hand, cutting off Mack-enzie's sentence. 'There has been no discussion about anything except that last time we rushed into things far too quickly and this time, well, Flynn wants to take his time.'

'Are you two sharing…a room?' Bergan asked coyly.

'No. Again, he wants to take it slowly.'

'But you have told him about your past? He knows who your parents were?' Sunainah asked quietly.

'Yes.'

'Then it is good he is wanting to take it slowly.' Su-nainah nodded in approval. 'I am liking this Flynn Ja-mieson more and more.'

'But it would be great if we could get to know him better,' Mackenzie pointed out.

'Uh-oh.' Bergan rolled her eyes. 'I'd know that organising look anywhere. Warning. Warning. Cul-de-sac crew gathering imminent.'

Reggie laughed. 'I think it would be great for Flynn to get to know the rest of you much better, too.'

'No doubt Elliot, Richard and John will want to take him under their wing, teach him the dos and don'ts of dealing with the four of us?' Mackenzie clapped her hands. 'Oh, it's just the way I've always wanted it. The four of us, living near each other, helping each other, being a family together.'

Reggie wanted to point out again that nothing was permanently fixed between herself and Flynn but one look at Mackenzie's brightly smiling face and Reggie swallowed the words. For now she could keep her concerns to herself. Like Flynn, she wanted to take things slowly, make sure that they were both on the same page, that they wanted the same things out of life.

For example, she had no idea whether he planned to live in the Sunshine Coast once his contract at the hospital had ended. Did he want to have children in the future? Did he want to travel? How did he see their working relationship? Did he want to work at a different hospital from her? When would he be ready to take their relationship to the next level? Was he still in contact with his father? Did he want her to meet his father? What had really happened between himself and Violet, his ex-wife?

When they'd been together in the Caribbean, he'd occasionally spoken of Violet and his family. 'I'm an only child and so is she,' he'd once told Reggie as they'd walked hand in hand along the beach, admiring the breathtaking sunset.

'Our mothers are the closest of friends and although Violet is a few years younger than me, the two of us have sort of been raised together. We went to the same schools. I was told to look out for her. We played together when we were young. We celebrated birthdays and Christmases with each other's families.'

'So she's just a friend?' Reggie had asked, slightly jealous of the wonderful life he was describing.

'Yes. Nothing more than a friend,' he'd confirmed.

And yet not too long after they'd had that conversation he'd been married to Violet. Now that he'd told her the true circumstances surrounding that union, Reggie still had questions. Was he still friendly with Violet? If so, *how* friendly? Or had their forced marriage been the undoing of a lifetime of friendship? Was that why he didn't talk about her much?

That evening, as they sat watching an old movie together, Reggie really wanted to ask him about Violet, find out some of the answers to the questions that were spinning around in her head, but every time she opened her mouth to speak, she found the words simply wouldn't come out. Surely if he was still in close contact with Violet he would have said something. Wouldn't he? Perhaps the fact that he hadn't spoken much about her indicated their marriage had indeed wrecked the friendship and now the two of them were estranged.

'What am I supposed to do?' she asked Mackenzie as the two of them put the final touches on the ballroom, ready for tomorrow night's Christmas auction. They'd worked closely with the event co-ordinator and she had to admit that the room did indeed look incredibly festive, with green and red tinsel around the place, twinkle lights and a large Christmas tree in the corner. Still, they were responsible for the table decorations and as they'd spent the last few weeks making them, as well as getting people to donate things for the auction. But no matter how many great items were up for bidding, the bachelor auction was most definitely the highlight of the night.

'You're supposed to talk to him,' Mackenzie told her. 'If you want to know about Violet, just ask him. He'll tell you.'

'It's not that I don't trust him,' Reggie began, and Mackenzie raised one eyebrow in question. 'OK.' She spread her arms wide. 'So perhaps I do have a few trust issues. I just want to be sure, this time, that he's not going to up and leave me again. I won't be able to live through the pain a second time. I just won't survive.'

'And you think he's still in touch with Violet?'

'He has to be. Their families are connected and yet he's said nothing about seeing his father at Christmas, or—'

'OK. OK,' Mackenzie interrupted, and put her hands on Reggie's shoulders. 'The only way for you to get rid of this stress and anxiety you're heaping on yourself is to talk to him.' Mackenzie's phone rang and she stared at Reggie for a moment longer before answering it.

'You're right. You're right. I know you're right,' Reggie said, more to herself than to her friend. 'I'll talk to him about it tonight. He'd be open to the discussion...' She bit her lip. 'I hope.'

Mackenzie finished her call. 'That was John.'

'Emergency?'

Mackenzie grinned. 'Yes, but not of the medical kind. Ruthie's having a sleepover at a friend's house and my husband *needs* me.' She waggled her eyebrows up and down and Reggie couldn't help but laugh.

'Then you'd better get out of here.'

'I can stay and help you finish up here and—'

'Just go. You're lucky enough to have a husband who is crazy about you, so don't go keeping him waiting.'

Mackenzie hugged her friend close. 'Thanks, Reggie.'

Reggie sighed as Mackenzie went, going through the motions of setting up the rest of the table centrepieces before standing back and surveying the room. It looked fantastic. The auction night would be wonderful. They were going to raise a lot of money and she was prepared to pay top dollar for Flynn. No way in the world was she letting Ingrid Brown or any other woman secure the auction prize of a dinner date with the man she loved.

'I'm looking forward to winning you at the auction,' she'd told him the previous night. 'Then I'll have my very own slave.'

'Hey, that's not the terms of the contract. Whoever wins the auction gets to have dinner with me. That's it.' He'd shaken his head and waggled his finger at her. 'No one said anything about slave duties.'

Reggie had playfully slid one hand up his arm and then walked the fingers of her other hand up his chest, and Flynn's grin had widened. 'That depends on what you classify as *slave duties.*'

'Hmm.' He'd accepted the kiss she'd placed on his lips. 'I guess it does.'

After that, they didn't talked much for a while, the two of them completely absorbed in each other, but when things started to get a little heated, Flynn was the one to put on the brakes. 'You make it very difficult to take our time and to go slowly with this relationship,' he murmured against her lips. 'Especially when you are so incredibly delectable and addictive,' he continued, pressing kisses to her neck.

'Likewise,' she returned, plunging her fingers into

his hair and bringing his head back so their lips could meet once more. 'It's difficult, Flynn. I want you so much.'

'I know.' He pressed his mouth to hers, slowing things down before lying next to her on the soft rug on the living-room floor. He continued to hold her in his arms, the two of them just lying there. 'I like just… being with you. There's no stress or tension or pressure to be something I'm not. I can be myself with you and you can be yourself with me, and all of that means more to me than anything, Reg.'

He levered himself up onto one elbow and looked down into her beautiful face. 'I don't want you to think I take you for granted. I know what we have between us is rare and unique and incredibly special and I just don't want to mess it up.'

Reggie grinned. 'Slow it is, then.'

'It's the right thing for both of us,' he remarked, before looking past her and frowning.

'What's wrong?' she asked, a frisson of concern churning within her belly.

'Huh?'

'You're frowning. Is there anything I can help you with?'

The frown cleared at her words. 'Nothing's wrong.'

'Really?' Reggie shifted her head so she could see him better. 'Is it your father?'

Flynn shrugged one shoulder. 'I haven't seen or spoken to him in over three years and most of the time I'm fine with that but…'

'Christmas can highlight the fact that families are estranged.'

'Exactly.'

'What did you used to do at Christmas?'

'He'll hire caterers, hold a huge, lavish affair at his house with lots of people he doesn't know, as well as all the people who work in his companies. They'll all get drunk, make mistakes by sleeping with the person they like least and wake up the day after with a multitude of regrets.'

'Sounds like a riot,' she remarked blandly, rubbing her fingertips over the frown lines on his forehead, wanting to do whatever she could to ease them. 'Do you want to see your father?'

'No.' The answer was immediate. 'I've tried in the past to make contact with him and he hasn't appreciated it one little bit. As far as he's concerned, he has no son.'

'Oh, Flynn.'

He swallowed and she knew if she pressed him on the issue he might clam up. She knew what it was like to be disowned by people who were supposed to love you. The wealthy really did have their own set of rules. It was sad that they lived by them. 'So this year,' he said after a moment, 'I am definitely looking forward to starting a new Christmas tradition.'

'Really?'

'With you.'

'Yes.' She kissed him.

'And no doubt the cul-de-sac crew have their big parties and present-giving? Mackenzie and Bergan are already swamped with family. I met Richard's parents yesterday.'

And so they discussed plans for Christmas Day, Reggie more than pleased that it appeared he wanted to spend the day with her. She wanted to ask about Violet. About whether he'd wanted to see her, but she didn't. And now, looking at the festive ballroom, looking perfect for the hospital's Christmas party, she wanted to push aside that one niggling fear of doubt that kept telling her that things seemed too perfect.

'Good things don't happen to me,' she whispered to herself as she headed out into the late-afternoon sunshine. It was such an odd feeling. She had good friends around her. She had a place to stay while all the insurance claims on her apartment were settled. Her neighbours were more than comfortable in the temporary housing Flynn had been generous enough to not only find for them but pay for them. He'd also insisted on remaining anonymous, telling Reggie he didn't need people to be beholden to him.

And above all, she had Flynn back in her life, back wanting to be with her, back wanting a future with her? Hopefully that was the case. Why else would he be insisting they take things slowly? Why else would he be insisting they start their own traditions together?

As she headed down the street towards the hospital, which was only two blocks away, Reggie wondered whether she should tell Flynn that she loved him. Would her declaration change things? Was it what he was waiting to hear before they took their relationship to the next level?

'Oh, why aren't these things as easy as a hernia repair?' she mumbled, as she stopped at the pedestrian lights and pressed the button. She looked down the side street, seeing a family—a mother, a father and little boy—chatting together. A family. A normal family. It was something she'd longed for all her life. The man had his back to her but the woman, with her long blonde hair falling slightly over her face, was folding the stroller and putting it into the boot of her fancy car. The boy was clinging to his father, clearly a little sleepy and more than content to relax in the big, trusty arms that held him.

Reggie sighed, instinctively knowing that Flynn would make a wonderful father. Wouldn't it be nice if that were them? Having spent a lovely day out together, looking forward to heading home and relaxing. Normal people. Normal lives.

The woman closed the boot then held her hands out for the boy. As the man turned to hand the child over, Reggie saw his face. His smiling face—the face smiling at the blonde-haired woman.

'Flynn.' The whispered word left her lips in utter disbelief. The pedestrian lights turned green. Reggie didn't move. Couldn't move as she watched the woman say something to Flynn, both of them laughing brightly. Flynn kissed the little boy and the boy kissed him back, both of them clearly comfortable with each other.

Part of Reggie's mind was racing, panicking, trying to figure out what it was she was seeing, while the other part of her mind was stuck, standing still in stunned shock. Who was the woman? Who was she? Reggie thought back to all those years ago, of the times when she'd read the glossy society mags…and then she remembered where she'd seen that blonde woman. She'd seen her dressed as a bride, she'd seen her looking lovingly up at Flynn as he'd stood beside her—the groom.

The woman was Violet. His ex-wife. After Violet had put the little boy into the car, she'd turned, hugged Flynn close and then pressed a warm kiss to his lips.

Reggie's heart was breaking. It was breaking again. *Flynn* was breaking her heart all over again…and yet it was impossible for her to move. Misery and despair flooded her as the pedestrian lights turned red. Stop. Don't walk. Don't move. Your life is over.

She waited, knowing the inevitable was about to happen, and her heart started pounding out a scared tattooed rhythm against her chest as he began to turn in her direction. In another moment he would see her standing there…watching him.

She shook her head. She didn't want to see him. Didn't want him to see her. Run and hide. *Flee!* Her mind was starting to scream commands at her body but her legs didn't seem able to follow their lead as she remained exactly where she was.

He waved goodbye to the boy in the car, the boy who looked just like him, the boy who was definitely old enough to be his son. If Flynn had a son, why on earth hadn't he told her about him? Was it a condition of his freedom from his father? To hand over access to his son? Was Violet supposed to be in contact with him?

She knew her mind was going into overdrive, clutching at straws to try and make some sort of sense from what she was seeing. The traffic around her was starting to slow again and she became peripherally aware of other people joining her at the pedestrian lights, pressing the button and waiting beside her.

Could they hear the wild pounding of her heart? Could they feel her pain? Her terror? The one man she'd loved with all her heart had hurt her, not once but twice!

He was turning in her direction, taking a few steps up the street as he continued to wave to the car as Violet indicated and pulled out from the kerb. Reggie couldn't breathe. It was impossible to drag air into her lungs because within a split second he would see her…standing there…watching him betray her.

The moment their gazes met, it was as though the world seemed to stop spinning. Flynn looked confused, then shocked, his eyes widening. His step faltered for a split second, as though he was deciding what it was he should do. He'd just been caught kissing his ex-wife! What would he do?

The next instant he increased his speed, walking with purpose, a determined look in his eyes.

Reggie shook her head and took a step back, even though he was still quite a way away from her. The traffic around her slowed and then the pedestrian lights turned green. The people around her started walking across the street. She looked from the lights back to Flynn and shook her head. Now that she'd actually moved, her body seemed capable of more reaction. Her eyes immediately flooded with tears and her lower lip began to quiver.

'Reggie!'

She shook her head, panic rising within her. She couldn't face him. She didn't want to hear his reasoning, his excuses. All her life people had reasoned with her, provided excuses for the terrible things that had happened to her, and now the one man in the world she'd started to trust, the one man who had captured her heart, was going to break it once again.

'Reg! Wait. I can explain!' His words reached her ears but she brought her hands up, covering them, blocking out his words as she turned and raced across the road just in time. In another instant the traffic started up again, leaving Flynn on one side of the road and Reggie on the other.

Worlds apart, or so it seemed. Flynn had told her she could trust him, that he was different from all the others, but it appeared he'd been lying to her.

Brushing the tears from her eyes so she didn't trip over, Reggie made her way down the street, almost running towards the hospital as though it was her one and only lifeline. The instant she rounded the door, she headed down the stairs, needing to hide herself away, needing to find a place where she could expel the pain from her heart, where she could drag in a cleansing breath, where she could start to make a plan to regroup.

Could she recover from a broken heart yet again? She didn't think so.

CHAPTER ELEVEN

'REGGIE?' BERGAN'S VOICE came over the phone when Reggie had answered the call. 'Where are you?' She'd already rejected several calls from Flynn's cellphone. He was the last person she felt like talking to. How could he? How could he do this to her? She'd opened up her heart, her soul. She'd bared her pain, her horror to him and this was how he thought it was OK to behave? To betray her? No. No. No. The pain in her heart intensified and she choked on another sob.

'Reggie?' Bergan spoke again and it was only the evident concern in her friend's voice that prompted Reggie to answer.

'What?' There was no disguising the tears and pain in her voice as she sniffed and snuffled.

'Where are you? What's happened?' Bergan's tone was insistent and filled with that protective love Reggie had relied on more than once throughout the course of their friendship.

'I… Flynn…' Reggie tried to get the words out but it appeared it was impossible. She'd only just managed to calm herself down, thinking she might be ready to call one of her friends to come and get her, but now that she actually had to put into words what she'd seen,

Reggie found the wave of anguish was washing over her once more.

'He was here in A and E, looking for you, and was quite frankly beside himself with worry. What's happened?'

'Is…is he still th—?' She couldn't finish the sentence, the panic that he might be listening in to this conversation making Reggie skittish again.

'No. I sent him away.'

'Good.' She sighed with relief. 'Good.'

'Where are you?' There was more insistence, more concern in Bergan's words than before.

'When things go belly up, go down, down, down and get as far away as possible.'

'Ah…taking a leaf out of Sunainah's book, eh? Hiding in the basement beneath the stairs. It's a good place, I have to admit. OK. Stay put. I'll be there soon.'

'Don't tell him.' The words were out before she could stop them. 'I don't want to see him. I don't want to speak to him. *Ever*.'

'Relax, Reggie. I've got your back.' With that Bergan disconnected the call and Reggie sat beneath the stairwell in the hospital basement, hugging her knees to her chest.

It was the same place she'd found Sunainah, so long ago now, when Sunainah's life had looked as though there was no possibility for a happy ending. Now her friend was happily married to Elliot, the two of them enjoying being parents to Elliot's wonderful children and even talking about having some of their own. Things had worked out for Sunainah but Reggie couldn't see any possibility of things working out for her and Flynn, not now that he'd betrayed her.

Honesty. That was the main thing she needed out of

any relationship. Pure and open honesty, and stupidly she'd thought Flynn had thought the same way. Cover-ups, lies and deceit played no part in her life. Hadn't he understood that?

So why on earth had he been warmly kissing his ex-wife?

He'd been holding a little boy who looked just like him and who he appeared to love very much. Reggie had been able to see that clearly in his eyes. Did Flynn have a son? If so, why hadn't he told her about him? Why had he felt the need to keep secrets from her? Not to trust her? To hurt her by betraying her yet again?

She'd been a fool to think that things were looking up for her, that finally she might be able to find the elusive happiness she'd been searching for all her life. Over and over again people came into her life and they let her down. If it weren't for Mackenzie, Sunainah and Bergan showing her it was indeed possible to trust, Reggie would have given up long ago and allowed the spirit of pessimism and depression to invade her heart.

She searched her pockets for a tissue and eventually found one, dabbing her eyes and blowing her nose, knowing she could well play the part of Santa's lead reindeer with her red face.

'Reggie?'

Finally she heard Bergan's voice echo down the stairwell and held her breath, her eyes wide as she listened to the footfalls on the stairs. Were there two people coming down? Had Flynn been lurking in the shadows? Watching Bergan? Following Bergan, knowing she would lead him to where she was hiding?

'Reggie? I'm alone,' Bergan said, as though answering her unspoken question.

'Are you sure?'

'Yes.' There was absolute certainty in Bergan's words and Reggie breathed out a sigh of relief as she wriggled out from her hiding spot and brushed herself off. The instant Bergan stood before her, Reggie threw herself into her friend's arms, fresh tears spilling forth. Bergan placated her, stroking her back as the gut-wrenching sobs started all over again.

'Here's a fresh pack of tissues,' Bergan eventually offered after a minute or two. Reggie eased back, knowing she must look a sight and immediately wiped her eyes and blew her nose. 'Flynn told me what happened.' Bergan spoke softly. 'He says it's not what you think.'

'How would he know what I think?' Reggie asked, a fresh bout of tears stinging in her eyes. 'He lied to me, Bergan. He kept asking me to trust him and I did and I told him all about my past and how people have constantly let me down—all my life—and now he's done it to me. Not once, but *twice*!' Her words were scattered, broken up between sobs and hiccups, her voice high and bordering on hysteria. *'Twice!'* She held up two fingers as though to confirm it. 'Why am I so stupid? Why do I let him do this to me?'

Bergan shrugged. 'I don't know, Reggie, but first things first. We need to get you out of here. I've left Richard in charge of A and E and I'm taking you—'

'Not to the cul-de-sac.' Her words were instant, her eyes flashing with insistent fire. 'You have people staying with you and so does Mackenzie and I don't want to be near Flynn. I just need space. I need to be able to breathe and to think things through and—'

'I understand and I know the perfect place for you to go. Somewhere safe.' Bergan held out her hand to her friend.

'You do?'

'Come on.' Reggie allowed herself to be led away by Bergan, but couldn't help the need to constantly look over her shoulder just in case Flynn was lurking around the corner. 'Relax. Flynn's gone. He left the hospital over half an hour ago. He said he had some things to organise.'

Reggie sighed with relief at knowing Flynn really wasn't on the hospital grounds and when she was safe in Bergan's car she rested her head back against the seat and closed her eyes, her head starting to pound. All she could see, all she could think about was the image of Violet and Flynn, kissing each other. It was as though it was burned into her memory and would remain there forever. At least the last time he'd broken her heart there had only been him telling her it was over—not the vision of him lip-smacked with his ex-wife! How could he have done that to her?

When Bergan stopped the car, Reggie found herself outside the new apartment block where Melva and her other neighbours were staying. The apartments Flynn had organised.

'Melva's place?' There was a hint of hope in Reggie's tone.

'What do you think?'

'This is perfect,' Reggie remarked, nodding. 'I haven't found the time to come and visit my neighbours since the fire and…' She looked at Bergan. 'This *is* just what I need. Some Melva therapy.'

'An escape,' Bergan remarked, smiling at her friend.

'Yes.'

'Go and spend time with Melva. I'm sure the evening nurse who comes to change the dressings on Melva's burns would love the night off, knowing you're going to be staying here for the night.'

'Of course I'll change Melva's dressings. That woman has always been there for me, from the first moment we met.'

'I know.'

'And it's all right with Melva?' Reggie checked as she undid her seat belt and alighted from the car. Her answer was to have her neighbour open the front door and come out to her, walking frame in front in order to steady her.

'Oh, Reggie. What a wonderful surprise. I was delighted when your young man called and said you were coming to stay.'

'My young…man?' Alarm bells instantly began to ring in Reggie's ears as she looked quickly at Bergan, whose answer was to simply shrug one shoulder and sigh.

'I can't take credit for thinking to bring you to Melva's. It was Flynn's idea. He said if you needed space then he would give you space.'

'Flynn organised all of this?' Reggie wasn't sure whether to feel betrayed by Bergan or happy that Flynn had realised she needed space. Darn him for being his usual thoughtful self. It made it even more difficult for her to remember the pain he was causing her. 'That is so like him,' she growled between gritted teeth. 'Why does he have to do something nice when he's hurt me so badly?'

'Perhaps he's trying to show you how much he cares.'

'Then he should care by *not* kissing his ex-wife.'

'Listen,' Bergan said, hugging her friend close and whispering in Reggie's ear. 'I think the man is crazy about you. Even Richard agrees. Flynn is head over heels in love with you.'

'Ha!' Reggie snorted. 'He's got a funny way of

showing it. By lying to me. By not telling me about…'
She stopped, closing her eyes on the memory that was
once more flashing before her eyes. 'You know what?
It doesn't matter. *I* want to see Melva. *I* want to spend
time with her, so that's what *I'm* going to do.'

'Good for you,' Bergan replied. 'Rest and relax. Get
rid of your anxious mind. Enjoy your day off tomorrow.
Sleep in. Watch TV. I'll see you at the hospital auction
tomorrow night.'

Reggie grimaced at these words. 'I don't know if I
want to go. I don't know if I want to see Flynn. It's too
soon, especially if he's trying to control my life from
afar.'

'Reggie.' Bergan smiled at her friend. 'He's not controlling anything. You are in complete control of all
your faculties. Just relax and think about tomorrow
when tomorrow comes.'

'Are you coming in for a cuppa, Bergan?' Melva
asked from the doorway. 'I've just bought some nice
new cups. They're very flash, bone china, and I spent a
bit more on them then I should have but then I decided
that after everything that's happened, I deserved a treat.
Did you know,' Melva continued, 'that apparently we
get paid a recovery allowance to help us buy new things
while we're waiting for the insurance money to come
through? I thought I'd be out of pocket for weeks but at
the moment I seem to have more money than I know
how to deal with.'

Reggie closed her eyes for a moment, delighted with
the beaming smile on her neighbour's face, knowing
instinctively that Flynn was the one who had provided
that allowance. Insurance companies didn't settle up
that quickly. He was using his wealth for the good of
others and her heart warmed at the thought.

Perhaps he *was* different from the other people who had allowed money and position to corrupt them. Deep down inside she knew Flynn wasn't like that. He didn't use people and lie to them. So why hadn't he told her about Violet? About the boy? Why hadn't he been able to trust her?

'No, thanks, Melva,' Bergan replied, her words snapping Reggie's attention back to the present. 'Just dropping Reggie off. I need to get back to the hospital.' She hugged her friend again and looked pointedly at her. 'Call me later if you want to talk.'

'No need to worry about that,' Melva said. 'Reggie and I are going to have a great ol' chin-wag, aren't we, love? Now, come on in. Ooh, look. Here's a delivery van pulling up. Good heavens, it's like Grand Central Station out here at the moment.'

Sure enough, the driver of the delivery van was soon walking towards them, a parcel in his hands.

'I'm looking for Reggie Smith?'

Reggie's eyes widened at that, then she frowned in confusion. 'Uh…that's me.'

'OK. If you could sign here.' He waited until she'd done as he'd asked, then handed over the parcel. 'You ladies have a lovely evening,' he said with a polite smile and just as quickly as he'd arrived, he disappeared.

'What is it?' Melva asked, and a stunned Reggie gave it a quick shake.

'I don't know.'

'Then come inside and we'll open it.' Melva turned to Bergan. 'Bye-bye, deary. Thanks for dropping her off. I'll take it from here.' Melva pointedly winked at Bergan, not being very subtle, but Reggie decided to let it go for now.

After waving goodbye to Bergan, Melva and Reggie

headed inside to see what exactly was in the package. 'There's no return address, except for a local department store.' Reggie closed the door and walked into the comfortable lounge room, remembering to admire the décor of the apartment.

'Ooh. A mystery.' Melva found a pair of scissors and handed them to Reggie so she could open it.

'Hmm.' Reggie looked slyly at the elderly woman. 'Is it really?'

Melva giggled as Reggie cut open the top of the parcel, then pulled out a toothbrush, a tube of toothpaste, a pair of soft satin pyjamas and a hairbrush and clean, new underwear that was scarlet.

'Now, *those* are far more expensive than my tea cups,' Melva remarked, before whistling, the noise making Reggie blush. 'Is there a note?'

'No, but I think we both know exactly who they're from.'

'They're from the same person who's found this furnished apartment, who's paying my allowance and who rang me, not half an hour ago and asked if it was all right for you to come and visit for the night.'

'What did he say?' Reggie asked softly.

'He said you'd had a shock and he wanted you to have some space and time to process everything. He thought spending some time with me, the closest person you have to a mother, might be good for you. I told him I was more like your grandmother but I knew what he meant.'

A lump formed in Reggie's throat as Melva recounted what Flynn had said to her. 'You know who he is, don't you,' she stated quietly.

'Of course, dear. I lived in Melbourne for many

years. I used to do private hairdressing for the likes of those people.'

Reggie's eyes widened at this news. 'So…do you know who I—?'

'Yes, dear.' Melva eased herself down into a comfortable high-backed armchair. 'I've known from the first moment I clapped eyes on you.'

'And yet you never said anything?' A lump welled in Reggie's throat.

'Why? What was the point in dredging up pain?' She shook her head. 'A person's past is their past. There's nothing they can do to change it. They can only learn from it and move forward into a better version of their future. If you get stuck in quicksand you either stay there, not caring that you can't get out, or you do something about it.' Melva looked at Reggie and nodded, pride in her voice. 'You were one of the strong ones. You were able to leave your past behind you, go to medical school, make something of your life, but sometimes…like with your young man…well, it just takes a little bit longer for people to figure things out. He had to get out of the quicksand and he could only do it for the right reasons.'

'Do you think *I'm* involved with those reasons?'

Melva chuckled. 'What do you think, ya silly goose?'

Reggie frowned, listening carefully to what Melva was saying. She knew the wise woman was right, even though the last thing Reggie wanted was to be rational about all this. Her emotions were mixing again, tumbling over each other in a mass of confusion.

It was true there was no way she could change what had happened in either her past or the one she'd shared with Flynn. The past was the past. She knew deep down inside he was a good man and while they'd both made

mistakes—him for leaving her and her for letting him—
it didn't change the fact that he'd hurt her.

Logically, she knew time and a bit of distance was
necessary for her to sort her thoughts out but emotionally she wanted to be mad at him, she wanted to hold
on to her anger. She wanted to continue being annoyed
with him, especially as he really did seem to know
her very well. He'd realised that her spending time
with Melva, away from him, away from Mackenzie,
Bergan and Sunainah—being with someone who was
completely impartial to all that had gone before—was
exactly what Reggie would need.

'Hmm,' she growled softly, the frown still marring
her forehead.

'Don't overthink things, Reggie. Sometimes you just
need to go with the flow.' Melva waved her hands in
the air.

Reggie sighed and turned her attention back to
Melva, the frown immediately disappearing. 'How did
you get to be so wise?' she asked.

Melva chuckled. 'I'm eighty-two years old, darling,
that's how. I've picked up a thing or two about this
whole game-of-life thing.' She sighed. 'Now, are you
going to make us a cup of tea in my new fancy cups
and start enjoying yourself or do I have to get cross
with you?'

Reggie instantly smiled as she stood to her feet. 'Tea
it is.'

Even though she'd had a lovely time with Melva, Reggie didn't sleep all that well. Her mind was constantly
churning with everything she knew about Flynn, trying
to piece together exactly what sort of man he was. Before yesterday she would have said he wasn't the type of

man to cheat on a woman but she'd seen the way money could corrupt even the most saintly of men.

If that little boy was his son, then it was something she would have to deal with if there was any hope of a future with Flynn. Did she want a future with Flynn? Her heart was saying yes, yes, yes, but her mind was saying no, no, no.

Then what of Bergan? Her strong, determined friend, who would stand like a guard with swords crossed to staunchly protect her from any enemy, had crumbled and gone along with the plan Flynn had put into place. She knew that happiness came from within and that she couldn't rely on someone else, couldn't hold them responsible for her own happiness, but she also accepted that to go through the rest of her life with Flynn by her side would, indeed, go a long way to making her happy.

She'd tried living without him before and it had been difficult. If things really weren't as they seemed, if she'd somehow grabbed the wrong end of the stick then perhaps…maybe…would she really be foolish enough to employ some small level of hope?

'Oh, Flynn,' she whispered over her cup of early-morning coffee as she stood looking out of Melva's kitchen window as the sun rose, shining its glorious light all around. The darkest little cracks and crevices changed from a dull grey to vibrant colour. The yellows, pinks, purples and blues. Slowly but surely it was as though the world was waking up, coming to life, wanting to celebrate the new day.

Wasn't that how she'd been since Flynn had returned to her life? Filled with colour? Wanting to celebrate life? She'd forced herself to become a bright and bubbly person, always seeing the glass as half-full rather than half-empty, always wanting to look on the bright side of things, always wanting to surround herself with happiness, but now she knew as an absolute certainty that without Flynn in her life, that's all her life would ever be—forced happiness.

'Good morning, dear,' Melva said as she shuffled into the kitchen, the walking frame supporting her. 'Oh, good. You've already made the coffee.'

'I was going to bring you a cup but I confess to being sidetracked by the glorious sunrise.'

Melva nodded as Reggie quickly fixed her a cup. 'Let's go out onto the balcony and watch it together.' This they did and once they were seated, Melva asked her, 'So what have you decided?'

Reggie's quirky smile was instant. 'You know me too well.'

Melva chuckled but waited patiently for Reggie's answer.

'I think that I at least…I need to hear what he has to say before I can make any other decision.'

Melva snorted at this. 'Really? I think you've decided more than that.'

'What do you mean?'

'This isn't just about listening to the man, Regina.'

'It's not?'

'No.' Melva shook her head. 'What is wrong with you young people these days?' She put her coffee cup down on the table. 'I think it's great you want to listen to him, darling, but this is also crunch time.'

'Crunch time?' It was Reggie's turn to shake her head. 'I don't—'

'Do you love him?'

'Er…I…'

'It's a simple question, Reggie. Yes or no?'

Reggie swallowed. 'Yes.'

'So no matter what he might say to you, you're willing to face the consequences? Fight for him? Move heaven and earth to ensure the two of you stay together this time?'

Reggie's heart fluttered with excited fear. What if Flynn told her that the little boy was his son? Would she be able to accept that? Was she willing to be a part of his son's life? What if Flynn still had a lot of wealthy friends? Would she be able to spend time with them? Melva was right. Was she willing to fight for Flynn? To make sure that his life and her life were intertwined together—forever?

'Yes,' she replied again. 'I am.'

Melva's grin was wide as she nodded her head, as though encouraging Reggie to continue.

'I need Flynn in my life.' Reggie said the words more to herself than to Melva. 'I know I can survive without him, I've done it for the past six years, but I'm not sure if I want to just survive anymore. I've been doing that for most of my life—surviving. I want to be happy, Melva.' Her chin wobbled as she spoke the words and tears immediately sprang to her eyes. 'I want Flynn.'

Melva chuckled and leaned over to drape her frail arm around Reggie's shoulders. 'That's my girl.'

Feeling happier now that the decision had been made, Reggie had a cleansing shower, realising she would need to head out to the shops at some point to find something to wear to tonight's auction. She surveyed the bright scarlet underwear Flynn had sent as part of her overnight care package. No doubt he'd called one of the department stores where they'd gone shopping last week, asking one of the personal shoppers to gather a few things together and courier them to Melva's apartment.

At least she hoped that's what had happened because

even thinking about Flynn, standing in the lingerie section, searching for the perfect matching set of underwear for her…and such a delightfully wicked colour as well…made her cheeks suffuse with colour.

Would he take the time to personally do such a thing for her? Had he left the hospital and gone straight to the department store? He had told Bergan he had things to organise. Had he gone to such great lengths *just* for her?

And that wasn't all. During the course of the morning the doorbell rang twice and each time Reggie's heart pounded with scared excitement at the thought that it might be Flynn. Instead, there were more parcels being delivered, the first a small but perfect Christmas tree, along with a box of decorations. There was a note with it that simply said, 'Enjoy your day.'

A few hours later, once they'd erected the tree and dressed it with baubles and tinsel, the second package arrived.

'This really *is* like Christmas.' Melva giggled as Reggie signed for the parcel. This one, though, wasn't like the others. It was a long dress bag, with a smaller box inside. When she opened it, both she and Melva gasped. There, inside, was the most beautiful scarlet-coloured dress, perfect to match the underwear she presently had on beneath her new pyjamas. The bodice was tastefully embroidered with beads and a few sequins, the skirt was full and came to just below her knee. The small box at the bottom of the bag contained a perfect pair of matching shoes.

'Good heavens. This must have cost hundreds.'

'And then some,' Reggie murmured, instantly falling in love with the dress. It would be wrong of her to accept it, wouldn't it? Was Flynn trying to lavish gifts on her in order to buy her forgiveness?

'I should send it all back. The dress, the under-wear—'

'But not the decorations. Look how homely they make this new apartment look,' Melva said instantly.

Reggie surveyed the brightly coloured room and nod-ded in agreement.

'And why should you send it all back?' Melva con-tinued. 'The man isn't trying to buy you off, Reggie. You're far too strong for him to even attempt it. All he's doing is showing you how much he appreciates you. He's wooing you. For heaven's sake, girl, let the man be romantic. Now, off you go to the spare room and try on that dress. I want my own personal fashion parade of dress and shoes so we can decide on your hair and make-up—which I'll do for you. Now go. Shoo.'

She did as Melva had bidden her and they had a lovely time deciding on make-up and exactly how she should wear her hair. When the doorbell rang a third time, Reggie was all in a dither. Dressed in her pyjamas again, she almost raced to the door, filled with excite-ment to see what Flynn might be sending her *this* time.

When she opened the door, expecting to see a de-livery man standing there, waiting for her to sign for the next parcel, she almost tripped over her own feet to see Flynn.

'Flynn!'

She stared at him and he stared at her, both of them drinking in the sight of each other as though they'd been starved for years.

'Hello, Reg.'

'Uh...' She was at a total loss for words, unsure whether to invite him in or just stand there, or whether she should change into her clothes or thank him for all the gifts or... 'What do you want?' she blurted, instantly wishing her words hadn't come out sounding so confronting.

'I...um...' Flynn looked down at his hands, as though completely forgetting why he was here. It was then he seemed to realise he was holding a thick white envelope. 'I wanted to deliver this one. In person.'

'Oh, yes. Sorry.' Manners and a smidgen of coherent thought began to return. 'Er...thank you for all the—'

'It's fine.' He waved away her words with a hint of veiled embarrassment. 'I actually wondered if I could... read this to you.'

'Read it?' He was clearly nervous and it only made him seem more endearing. It was difficult, seeing him standing there—looking incredibly sexy in his blue denim jeans and pale blue shirt, casual but, oh, so delicious—really difficult to remember that just yesterday afternoon she'd seen him kissing another woman.

'Yes.' He dragged in a breath, as though pulling himself together. 'I have a lot of things I'd like to say to you, Reg, and all I ask is that you listen. I'm not looking for an answer or anything. No pressure. Just...please...will you listen?'

Reggie nodded and indicated for him to come inside but he shook his head. 'Here is good.' And without further ado he flicked open the envelope and pulled out a few sheets of paper. 'I wrote everything down, not only so I didn't forget the important things I need to say, because heaven knows that when I'm around you, Reg, my mind tends to turn to mush and all I can think about is holding you close and...' He trailed off and found himself staring at her yet again.

Didn't she have any idea just how adorably perfect she looked in those pyjamas? All soft and cuddly and so *his* Reggie?

'Anyway,' he went on, giving himself another mental shake. 'Here goes.' He cleared his throat. 'Oh, and I'd appreciate it if you didn't interrupt. Just let me get it all out.'

'OK.'

'Good.' He paused, then launched right in. 'Dear Reg.'

'Strong beginning,' she murmured.

'No interruptions.' He glared at her and she nodded again. He tried again. 'I want to apologise for not telling you more about my divorce. I guess as it's a topic I've learned not to discuss in public, I keep forgetting you don't know what really happened all those years ago. Rest assured that Violet and I are just friends.' He stopped and looked directly into her eyes. *'Friends,'* he reiterated, before going back to reading his letter.

'We've always been better friends than anything else. She is also happily married to my cousin, Colin. The child you saw me holding, Ian, is their son.'

'He's not your son?' Reggie whispered, hope filling her voice as he continued to read further.

'Violet and I should never have allowed ourselves to be bullied into the marriage, especially as she'd been in love with my cousin all along. She had broken off her relationship with him, just as I had done with you. Duty and family and all that guff was rammed down our throats and so we did as we were told, desperately trying to make a go of a marriage but instead only succeeding in making each other—and you and Colin—miserable.

'Violet and I secretly separated very soon after the marriage, more than happy to live our own lives, and it was then she began to see Colin again. When she fell pregnant, we all decided it was best to end the farce so that Violet and Colin could stand a chance of being a proper family unit.

'We all knew none of our parents would be pleased with the outcome but we did what we had to and now not only have they had five wonderful years together but Violet just told me that she's pregnant again with their second child. That was why she wanted to see me, to tell me the news in person. Unfortunately, Colin is overseas at the moment and wasn't able to join us.

'Reg, please believe me when I say that there is nothing romantic between Violet and myself. It is *you* I am most desperately in love with and it is *you* I wish to spend the rest of my life with.'

Reggie gasped and covered her mouth with her hand as he looked into her eyes.

'My heart has *always* been yours and I was a fool to have let you go once. I won't make that same mistake again.' Flynn was no longer reading from the page but instead was staring intently into her eyes. 'I love you, Reg. More so now than I did six years ago.'

She wasn't sure what to do, what to say. What was she supposed to do? She did love him back with all her heart and she wanted desperately to tell him, to let him know that he wasn't standing out on that big scary ledge of emotion all on his own, but somehow, for some strange reason, she couldn't get any of the words past her lips and her feet seemed permanently glued to the spot.

'I know this is a lot to take in,' Flynn continued, clearly not expecting any sort of response from her. 'Hence why I've written everything down. Take this letter, Reg. Read it over and over. Process it. Take your time. Don't rush but, please, believe me when I say that at the moment there's only confusion between us because that's all it is—a silly misunderstanding, and I hope my words have helped clear all that up.

'I'm really looking forward to seeing you tonight at the auction and one simple look from you, a gesture, a word even, will let me know whether or not you accept my apology and my love.'

Then, as she stood there, she watched him fold the papers, putting them back into the envelope with his clever, sure fingers. He held the envelope out to her and with numb fingers she took it...watching in surprise as he bowed his head to her then turned and walked away.

Reggie blinked, several times, wondering if she was still lying in bed, dreaming. Had she fallen and hit her head and was hallucinating? The envelope in her hands was evidence that it was neither and after she'd somehow managed to get her body to function yet again she closed the door, then slumped down into a chair, trying to take in everything that had just happened.

Flynn loved her. Flynn had just stood there, before her, declaring his love for her, letting her know that not only did he love her now but that he'd *always* loved her and always would. He was hers. His love was hers to have...if she wanted it.

'I do. I do want it.'

And yet he hadn't pressured her, hadn't come inside, hadn't talked at her, but instead had read the love letter out loud, sharing with her his thoughts and deepest emotions. He hadn't wanted anything from her, hadn't demanded any sort of response, hadn't forced her into anything.

'But I want him. I love him.' As though it was just too much for her to contain, she raced back to the door and flung it open, staring out into the street to try and see if he'd really left, but there was no sign of him.

'What's going on?' Melva called. 'Is there *another* person at the door?'

Reggie headed back inside and sat down again, surprised to find tears of happiness streaming down her face, a wide grin on her lips. She brushed the tears aside, her heart lifting in complete and utter delight to know that Flynn loved her, that he still loved her, that he'd *always* loved her. She laughed out loud, unable to believe how light and glorious it was to be loved back by the person you loved.

She unfolded the letter and read it again, just to reassure herself that this was really happening, that this was really true. He really *did* know her so well, wanting to ensure she wasn't pressured in any way, and that knowledge made her love him all the more.

'But he doesn't know I love him.' The words tumbled out of her mouth in a rush and she looked around anxiously for her phone. With trembling fingers she dialled his number, heart pounding wildly against her chest as she waited for it to connect. She wasn't quite sure what she was supposed to say; her mind had gone blank. The phone switched through to his voicemail, which meant he was probably driving. She waited for the message to end but when it was time to say something she opened her mouth to tell him that she loved him back, that she loved the dress and the other presents he'd bestowed on her, that she couldn't wait to see him tonight, that she was sorry for being such an insecure ninny and having a big freak-out…but no words came out of her mouth.

She quickly disconnected the call and realised what she must do. She must look her absolute best for tonight. Let Flynn see for himself just how much she loved him. She stood and checked the clock.

'Only three hours to get ready! Come on!'

* * *

Flynn stood, dressed in a tuxedo, not caring if he was slightly overdressed for tonight's auction or not. He wanted to look his absolute best when he saw Reggie, hoping amongst hope that his gifts and his letter of explanation, his letter of love, had proved to her that he loved her and that she could trust him. He fiddled with his tie as he stood near the rear of the small stage.

So far, the night had been going for a good twenty minutes and there was still no sign of Reggie. Was she coming? Had something happened? Perhaps he should have organised for a car to pick her up but then he thought she might consider that too controlling and the last thing he wanted was for her to think him controlling. He wanted to cherish her, adore her and love her for the rest of her life, and as he rubbed his sweaty palms down his trousers again, checking the door for the hundredth time, almost wishing her to burst through, he heard his number being called.

'And next up we have bachelor number five. Ladies, he's the latest addition to Sunshine General's surgical department. Please welcome Flynn Jamieson,' Mackenzie, who was the MC for the evening, announced into the microphone. Flynn looked at Mackenzie as if to ask where Reggie was. Mackenzie's answer was to shrug apologetically as Flynn took centre stage, standing beneath the plastic mistletoe hanging from the ceiling.

'Who would like to get the bidding started?' Mackenzie asked, and wasn't surprised when a plethora of hands went up, bids being called out. The previous bachelor had raised well over five hundred dollars and although Flynn wanted to raise money for the hospital, he didn't care if someone only bid five dollars, so long as that someone was Reggie. Where was she?

Mackenzie was taking bids, the price going past one hundred dollars, past two hundred, then three, then four. Up and up the price went, getting to seven hundred dollars. Ingrid Brown, the general surgical registrar, was in a battle with Clara from the outpatient department. Flynn couldn't believe someone would pay that much just to have dinner with him but then again it really was for a good cause.

'Do I have an increase on seven-fifty?' Mackenzie called. 'Seven-fifty going once. Seven-fifty going twice.'

'One thousand dollars!' came a loud female cry from the back of the room and everyone turned to look, turned to see Reggie standing there, dressed in the most glorious scarlet dress and matching shoes, her short dark hair spiked out a little, giving her a radiant appeal. People around her clapped; the hospital's administrator whooped with delight.

'Sold!' Mackenzie called, banging her gavel and ignoring Ingrid's frown. 'Step right on up, Reggie, and claim your Christmas bachelor,' she called. Reggie kept her gaze glued to Flynn's as she made her way through the ballroom, not tripping over a chair or a tablecloth and not overbalancing in the five-inch heels.

Soon enough, she was standing before him. 'Sorry I'm late,' were the first words out of her mouth. 'The taxi broke down and I had difficulty getting another one.'

'You look…' Flynn stared at her, not caring that everyone else was staring at the two of them. As far as he was concerned, there was no one else, no one else except Reggie. 'Stunning.'

Her smile increased as she looked up at him, then

motioned to the mistletoe above them. 'Look where you're standing, Dr Jamieson.'

He nodded and moved forward, sliding his arms about her waist and drawing her close. Wolf-whistles came from around them as well as a lot of cheering. Reggie didn't care. She wanted everyone in the world to know exactly how she felt about Flynn.

'Do you think we need it?' he asked, and she slowly shook her head from side to side.

'Thank you for your letter. It was perfect.'

'I hope you don't think I was trying to buy your affection by sending you the things I did.'

'I don't think that. I think you were trying to romance the woman you love.' She slid her hands slowly up his chest to link them behind his neck.

'I do. I do love you, Reggie, so very much. I've never loved anyone like I love you.'

'That's very good news,' she replied, her brand-new heels making her tall enough to lean in closer and line up her lips with his.

'It is?'

'Yes, because I've never loved anyone like I love you either.'

Finally, Flynn smiled at her, a small, secret smile that let her know that, finally, everything really would be all right. 'Marry me?' he asked, their lips only millimetres apart.

'Yes,' she replied instantly, and sealed their new deal with a kiss.

The room erupted into a frenzy of clapping and cheering as the two of them stood beneath the mistletoe, kissing each other with perfect delight.

'I'm sorry this proposal isn't as romantic as the last one,' he eventually said as they made their way out of the ballroom via a side door, not caring about anything at the moment but each other. With the moon above them, the stars twinkling in the night sky and Flynn's arms around her, holding her close, Reggie kissed his gorgeous, loving mouth.

'I like this one best, especially as I now own you.' He raised one eyebrow playfully at her words. 'Don't you realise that spread out over the next fifty years, you would only have cost me twenty dollars a year!'

'A definite bargain,' he returned, kissing her once again.

'Who said money couldn't buy love?' She giggled and allowed Flynn to keep on kissing her...forever.

EPILOGUE

'ARE YOU READY?' Sunainah asked.

Reggie stood dressed in a beautiful white wedding dress that had an asymmetrical split up the side, revealing a generous amount of her shapely legs. Ruffles seemed to be everywhere and as she looked at herself in the mirror, her three friends nodded in approval.

'That dress is *so* you,' Bergan said.

'I love it,' Reggie agreed. 'Almost as much as I love Flynn.' She giggled before turning to face her friends, looking at each of them in turn. She was surrounded by the people she loved and waiting for her in the communal garden area of the cul-de-sac stood the man of her dreams. 'Do you think I'm ready?'

Bergan, Mackenzie and Sunainah looked at each other for a split second before looking back at Reggie. 'Yes,' they said in unison.

'Only you would get married in a car park,' Bergan grumbled good-naturedly.

'It's not a car park. It's a lovely little garden that we all tend and love—'

'Which is right next to where guests usually park their cars when they come to visit,' Bergan added.

'Well, Mackenzie did want me to be part of the cul-de-sac crew and I think this definitely makes it official.'

'Just one more thing,' Sunainah said a moment later, and bent down to pull a rectangular parcel from a bag. It was wrapped in plain brown paper with no other adornments. 'This is for you.'

'Really?' Reggie accepted the parcel and looked at her friend in delight. 'I like presents.'

'I hope you will like this one.' Sunainah, Bergan and Mackenzie all grinned at each other as Reggie ripped the paper off with a touch of impatience and what she saw there made her stare at her friends in wonderment. There, in her hands, was a framed picture of herself and Flynn, standing on the beach in the Caribbean, sipping drinks with little umbrellas, the sun setting behind them.

'You told me to get rid of it but…I could not,' Sunainah confessed.

Reggie shook her head in wonder, then put the picture down and launched herself at her friends, hugging them all. 'Oh, this is perfect. This is the picture from our first real date. Oh, Sunainah, thank you for not listening to me and keeping it safe all these years. You three really are the best friends ever.'

'I am also pleased you decided not to wait and to get married *today*,' Sunainah added, as she set about fixing Reggie's dress once more. 'Christmas Day. Surrounded by everyone that you love most. It is perfect.'

'Yes.' Melva and her other neighbours would be part of the party and after the ceremony they were having a progressive Christmas wedding feast, going from one town house to the next. Reggie had wanted everyone to be included because everyone here was *her* family, the family she'd built around herself and the one in which Flynn now shared.

Since the auction Reggie had met Violet several

times, wanting to include her in the planning of the wedding.

'I'm so glad you and Flynn have finally found each other again,' Violet had said when the two of them had been alone. 'He loves you very much. Always has.'

'I know. The past is the past,' Reggie said. 'We can't do anything to change it but what we can do is accept it and plunge right on in to a newer and happier future.'

Violet had laughed. 'Flynn told me I'd like you and he was right. Thank you for making him happy.' The two women had hugged and when Flynn had returned, finding them laughing together, Reggie had seen true happiness reflected in his eyes. They weren't his future wife and his ex-wife, they were the love of his life and his surrogate sister…and they liked each other.

'OK,' Bergan said a moment later, bringing Reggie's thoughts back to the present. 'It's time to go because I have a feeling Flynn isn't going to wait too long for his bride to appear.'

'Right, girls,' Mackenzie said, marshalling her daughter Ruthie and Sunainah's daughter, Daphne, together. 'You come with me.'

'And boys,' Sunainah said, taking her son Joshua's hand and then offering her other hand to Violet's son, Ian, who Reggie had wanted to include in their wedding party. 'You are with me.'

'Out you come,' Bergan said, opening the front door to town house number three and waiting for the bride to precede her. As Reggie was an orphan, she'd decided she didn't need to be walked down the aisle by anyone. She would stand tall and walk towards Flynn by herself, offering herself to him, her three closest friends and the children behind her.

She accepted her bridal bouquet of bright red poinsettias from Bergan and smiled. 'Yes,' she said to them, before looking towards the garden where Flynn stood waiting impatiently for her. 'I'm ready. Ready for my normal, everyday life to begin. My life with Flynn.'

And with that, beaming brightly she walked towards the man who held her heart, giggling at his expression when he finally saw her, his jaw dropping in gobsmacked delight. Both Colin and Violet were standing in as his 'groomsmen' and with Richard, Elliot and John, as well as the rest of the extended families visiting for Christmas, it was almost difficult to find the wedding celebrant in the mix.

As soon as Reggie stood beside Flynn, she smiled up at him and gave a little shimmy, the ruffles on her dress shaking with the movement. 'Ready to get hitched?' she whispered.

'To you? Absolutely,' he replied, and took her hand in his. 'Now, this is a Christmas tradition I can get behind.'

Reggie laughed, unable to believe she could ever be this happy and it was all thanks to Flynn.

* * * * *

Mills & Boon® Hardback

December 2013

ROMANCE

Defiant in the Desert	Sharon Kendrick
Not Just the Boss's Plaything	Caitlin Crews
Rumours on the Red Carpet	Carole Mortimer
The Change in Di Navarra's Plan	Lynn Raye Harris
The Prince She Never Knew	Kate Hewitt
His Ultimate Prize	Maya Blake
More than a Convenient Marriage?	Dani Collins
A Hunger for the Forbidden	Maisey Yates
The Reunion Lie	Lucy King
The Most Expensive Night of Her Life	Amy Andrews
Second Chance with Her Soldier	Barbara Hannay
Snowed in with the Billionaire	Caroline Anderson
Christmas at the Castle	Marion Lennox
Snowflakes and Silver Linings	Cara Colter
Beware of the Boss	Leah Ashton
Too Much of a Good Thing?	Joss Wood
After the Christmas Party...	Janice Lynn
Date with a Surgeon Prince	Meredith Webber

MEDICAL

From Venice with Love	Alison Roberts
Christmas with Her Ex	Fiona McArthur
Her Mistletoe Wish	Lucy Clark
Once Upon a Christmas Night...	Annie Claydon

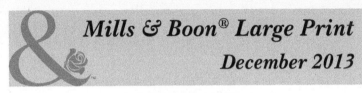

Mills & Boon® Large Print
December 2013

ROMANCE

The Billionaire's Trophy	Lynne Graham
Prince of Secrets	Lucy Monroe
A Royal Without Rules	Caitlin Crews
A Deal with Di Capua	Cathy Williams
Imprisoned by a Vow	Annie West
Duty at What Cost?	Michelle Conder
The Rings That Bind	Michelle Smart
A Marriage Made in Italy	Rebecca Winters
Miracle in Bellaroo Creek	Barbara Hannay
The Courage To Say Yes	Barbara Wallace
Last-Minute Bridesmaid	Nina Harrington

HISTORICAL

Not Just a Governess	Carole Mortimer
A Lady Dares	Bronwyn Scott
Bought for Revenge	Sarah Mallory
To Sin with a Viking	Michelle Willingham
The Black Sheep's Return	Elizabeth Beacon

MEDICAL

NYC Angels: Making the Surgeon Smile	Lynne Marshall
NYC Angels: An Explosive Reunion	Alison Roberts
The Secret in His Heart	Caroline Anderson
The ER's Newest Dad	Janice Lynn
One Night She Would Never Forget	Amy Andrews
When the Cameras Stop Rolling...	Connie Cox

1113 GEN STD LP

Mills & Boon® Hardback

January 2014

ROMANCE

The Dimitrakos Proposition	Lynne Graham
His Temporary Mistress	Cathy Williams
A Man Without Mercy	Miranda Lee
The Flaw in His Diamond	Susan Stephens
Forged in the Desert Heat	Maisey Yates
The Tycoon's Delicious Distraction	Maggie Cox
A Deal with Benefits	Susanna Carr
The Most Expensive Lie of All	Michelle Conder
The Dance Off	Ally Blake
Confessions of a Bad Bridesmaid	Jennifer Rae
The Greek's Tiny Miracle	Rebecca Winters
The Man Behind the Mask	Barbara Wallace
English Girl in New York	Scarlet Wilson
The Final Falcon Says I Do	Lucy Gordon
Mr (Not Quite) Perfect	Jessica Hart
After the Party	Jackie Braun
Her Hard to Resist Husband	Tina Beckett
Mr Right All Along	Jennifer Taylor

MEDICAL

The Rebel Doc Who Stole Her Heart	Susan Carlisle
From Duty to Daddy	Sue MacKay
Changed by His Son's Smile	Robin Gianna
Her Miracle Twins	Margaret Barker

Mills & Boon® Large Print
January 2014

ROMANCE

HISTORICAL

MEDICAL